FATHER'S DAY

A Military Sci-Fi Planet Tamers Novel

AUSTIN DRAGON

Published by Well-Tailored Books, California

Father's Day
(*A Military Sci-Fi Planet Tamers Novel*)

978-1-946590-20-6 (ebook)
978-1-946590-21-3 (paperback)

http://www.austindragon.com

Book cover design by Book Cover Zone
Printed in the United States of America

CONTENTS

INTRODUCTION 1

THE CREW 5

SATURN SPACE 6

The Neil deGrasse Tyson 8

The Call 54

Departure 64

The Uju Kauboi 76

Relieved of Duty 96

Incoming Call 106

Kauboi Halley 122

Final Orders 134

588 Achilles-2 148

Sightings 158

M.A.B. SPACE 171

The Belt Colonies 173

Uroboros Space Station 197

Wild Space 225

Beacon 237

USS Marines 253

The Nicolaus Copernicus 263

The Federation 279

The Sargasso Sea 295

The Randy Roger 311

Every Third Sunday of June 341

EPILOGUE 351

REVIEW REQUEST 359

ABOUT THE AUTHOR 363

INTRODUCTION

At 10:56 p.m. EST on 20 July, 1969, American astronaut Neil Armstrong landed on the moon and uttered the legendary phrase: "That's one small step for man, one giant leap for mankind."

Centuries have passed but that day has been taught in classes, both civilian and military, ever since. Humanity waits for the magic to be recreated. No one knows if the foot touching down on Titan will be that of a man or a woman, their native continent nor country, whether religious or not, whether soldier or scientist. However, there was no doubt what entity that pioneer would be from—Planet Tamers MN. Terraforming was about to go from science fantasy to government edict to scientist and military preparation to science fact.

Despite the magnitude of the historic operation, the year in space should have been like all the previous ones for First Lieutenant Joshua Halley. History meant nothing to a career soldier like him. It was one long operation. Long because it had been going on before he was born. Important to his outfit, yes, and to Earth too. But he took more notice of the commonplace of life, like the fact that he was a little older and a little grayer. He didn't care to notice his waistline, feeling that if he ignored it with conviction, any extra weight would simply go away. All in all, there shouldn't have been anything unique about the year, aside from the "elephant in the room." That was just how tin soldiers processed things. A mission was a mission. Humans continued to venture into the solar system, planting flags, and whole colonies where they could, confined to date to Luna and Mars. They launched endless probes into other systems as if there was anything else for us to see that our starscopes on Earth hadn't identified, analyzed, and cataloged decades or centuries earlier. Getting assigned to the Planet Tamers gig wasn't part of the norm of life. It was the opposite of normal. It was quite extraordinary and life-changing in every possible great way and Halley had settled in nicely. Life was good for the space soldier in today's military. All routine— until the day it wasn't.

A new hydra-class probe had been launched and that was all everyone was talking about. Anyone could hear the excitement of the crew and passengers before docking and egress. That meant the new orders would be on their way. The next phase of the mission would officially commence. Halley arrived on the Tyson but then got the call and everything changed.

Every human knows, or should know, that there's a membership club all of us will join against our will: the Club of Kids Whose Parents Have Died. If you're "lucky," it's after a long, long life and from natural causes. All clubs considered, it's not the worst of them. What did the comedian say: yep, we're all going to die one day. It's in the dictionary under Life. Probably at the top of worst clubs would be The Club of Parents Whose Kid Has Died Before Them.

Halley's wasn't that nightmare, but after that call he felt the emotion was so debilitating that it might as well have been. He'd always been told how tough of a grunt he was, even for an officer. The call nearly knocked him on his ass. It nearly made him cry. After that call, there was only one thing for him to do. He had lost his mother. He was damned if he was going to lose his father too. If there was even the smallest chance, he was going to find him. That was all there was to it. He didn't care if it cost him the Tyson job or his commission. The closest help was a year away! Seriously? He didn't care if he had to go AWOL. He was going to find him.

What a situation. Father's Day was just around the

corner.

"Hold on, Dad. I'm coming."

Titan would have to wait.

THE CREW

MILITARY SERVICES (USS Army)

RANK	LAST NAME	FIRST		CALL SIGN
LT (CPT)	Halley*	J. (Joshua/Josh)		Bogeyman
LT	Centaurus	C. (Carl)		Star Boy
SSG	Ogun	C. (Charles/Charlie)		God of War
CPL	Yuri	B. (Benjamin)		Crack Shot
PVT	Sirius	F. (Franco/Frank)		Leo the Lion
PVT	Superjovian	L. (Louis/Louey)		Minotaur
ADM	Antares	Z. (Zed)		Warlock

*Officer-in-Charge

SCIENCE SERVICES (USS Navy)

RANK	LAST NAME	FIRST		CALL SIGN
CPT	Ayla*	H.B. (Halle-Bopp)		Good News Girl
CDR	Cassiopeia	K. (Kez)		Sunrunner
LT	McAuliffe	C. (Carina)		Mack
Ensign	Rosen-bridge	A. (Aurora)		Symbiote
Ensign	Kirkwood	O. (Orion)		Sludge
TSGT	Klang	S. (Shaw)		Gremlin

*Officer-in-Charge

COMPANY: Planet Tamers MN – an Earth multinational consortium
SHIP: (cosmoship) NCS Neil deGrasse Tyson
CLASS/TYPE: Nautilus-class base cruiser
MISSION: *Operation Fairy Dancer*
Terraform Titan, the largest moon of Saturn!

SATURN SPACE

Chapter One

The Neil deGrasse Tyson

The NCS Neil deGrasse Tyson. Flagship of the Earth Alliance.

The Tyson was one of Mil-Sci's oldest scientific exploratory base cruisers and had been the pride of the Planet Tamers Multinational's (the Company) fleet for the better part of six decades. But to see the cruiser flying through space, one would swear it looked like it had launched yesterday: a large silver-blue rectangular passenger section with three gravity rings encircling the long main body at its front, center, and rear thirds; a tethered forward navigation and operations section; and, tethered at the rear, the revered Helios engine section. Modern physics wouldn't grant humans warp-drive, but with the Helios engine and proper trajectory mapping, a cosmoship could get from Earth to Saturn in just under two years—not eight. The ultra-classified space propulsion engine was a thing of beauty but it was also so massive as to be almost as large as the cruiser itself.

No one could ever accuse the Company of not spending its extremely lucrative profits on its ships, crew, and equipment. Clean, fast ships with the latest tech meant happy, loyal crews and even more company profits. It was why every scientist and soldier worth their atoms wanted to work for them, and the Company had its pick of the best of the best. It was why Planet Tamers MN had been awarded the coveted Titan terraforming contract over every other multinational and government agency on Earth. After centuries of fantasizing, talking, and preparing, humans finally meant business in turning another planetary body in the solar system into "Earth Two." With that single act, humans would go where no Terran life form had gone before: becoming a multi-planet species.

"Command, this is the NCS Merman. Requesting permission for docking."

"Merman, entry codes received. Permission for docking granted."

"Command, received and understood. Beginning docking approach now."

The Merman was a Dolphin-class shuttle, a favorite of the military for transporting squads and small cargo loads. Lieutenant Josh Halley stood two inches shy of six feet, but shuttles were too small to be equipped with gravity rings, so, at the moment, he floated weightlessly in the cockpit behind the two seated male pilots. As an Army military craft, all the men were in standard green, forever-creased, camouflaged, combat fatigues with field caps on their heads. Army and Navy didn't have the practically-bald "hairdos" of the Marines but men had to have close-cuts, especially at the sides, and hair never went past the shoulders for the women.

The two Army pilots were strapped in, but they all watched the final approach to dock with the Tyson. Halley steadied himself using one of the ceiling handholds. There was nothing unusual about the hop. All three enlisted men had hundreds of hours of space flight between them and could dock any vessel with their eyes closed but, complying with standard Mil-Sci protocol, the computers would do all the work. For final docking, Tyson Command took control of the Merman's propulsion and navigation computers. The vessel turned to its port side and continued forward for the final docking. The procedure was not just human-error-proof but stupid-human-error-proof. Halley's instructors in flight school often said that if humans became extinct, our pets and any stray animal off the street would have no problem driving and flying our vessels for themselves—no advanced evolution required.

Space was a peaceful place. Beautiful and hypnotic. The Tyson may have been a huge floating city to them, a triumph of humanity's creativity and craftsmanship, but to space it was unremarkable. Halley wondered if the cosmic intelligence he believed space possessed even registered the existence of supernovas and black holes. Was space truly endless? What did it matter? Their own solar system was more than enough for humankind. The cosmos was telling them: I'll let you see parts of me in all my vast splendor for you to dream your dreams to create, grow, and evolve. But be content with the corner I give you, as it is more than enough. You do not believe that now, but you will as your species matures.

Halley always watched the ship when docking as if it were his first time seeing her. No matter what name a cosmoship had—male or female—it was a "she." As old as it was, the Tyson remained the most advanced base cruiser that Earth had to offer. It was the largest cruiser with the largest Helios engine ever constructed. They called it a scientific exploratory vessel with its own military complement for defense but it was a floating city, "packed to the rafters" with a crew of four hundred and fifty—two hundred Navy personnel, two hundred Army personnel, and the remainder, "orphans," consisting of civilians and unaffiliated military-on-loan, like their new engineering officer. The reality was that the ship's largest function was not the science services or the military; it was what ship engineers called the triad: CO_2 production, water production, and waste management—air, water, and shit. If your spaceship couldn't manage those three functions, it would be a very short flight.

The three men's trained ears heard the separate click, seal, and pressurizing all at the same time. To the untrained ear the three distinct sounds would register as one. But each was critical and any one of them missing would trigger the loudest of warning alarms. Not unexpectedly, a steady green light shone on the cockpit display and around the shuttle's two doorways. Lieutenant Halley spun around and sailed through the air.

"See you inside, gentlemen," he said to the pilots.

"Will do, sir," they replied.

"Home sweet home, we return."

Scientists and soldiers rotated off-station when they wanted to, when their term was up, or for a cause so rare as to not even be mentioned. Techs rotated on and off all the time. With Tyson in deep space, a stopover at the space dock on Earth, Mars, or Luna was not an option. Therefore, the space dock was sent to them by way of a recently arrived platoon of the best techs Earth could find. The Tyson was already state-of-the-art but after a year and a half of nonstop work, the techs made it more cutting-edge. Planet Tamers spared no expense, as the Company's flagship would soon make history.

No one told him to do it but Halley accompanied the termed-out techs off the Tyson to their new ship back to Earth—a small Argonaut-class cruiser dispatched solely for them. The men and women had never had the pleasure of being chaperoned by a commanding officer before. They all had a good time and Halley enjoyed the brief respite from his normal duties. One of the perks of command: from time to time, the captain could do what they wanted.

He wasted no time in opening the main door. Waiting at the open bay door was the Tyson's receiving and tech crews. Dark blue-uniformed Navy personnel fully equipped with their tech cases stepped onto the shuttle with gravity boots. The techs would be on the shuttle for hours doing their inspection and maintenance. Halley exited with one large duffel bag over his shoulder, carrying another by the straps in one hand. With his free hand, he removed his head gear. As soon as he floated across an invisible line, the artificial gravity kicked in and he softly landed on his feet.

From the time any living thing set foot aboard the ship, they were under round-the-clock surveillance and monitoring by cameras and sensors. But before that, one had to be granted access by the ship's Receiving personnel, no matter who one was. Machines could check for biological and inorganic anomalies but, even as advanced as they were, it was still believed that only another human could properly evaluate mental ones.

"Welcome to the Tyson, sir," said a grinning Navy ensign in bluish camouflage fatigues. The young man began to salute.

"Please don't do that," Lieutenant Halley said. "I thought we're not doing cross-branch saluting nonsense anymore."

"Wartime only, sir?"

"Absolutely not, ensign. So enemy snipers know who all the officers are, who I am? I don't think so."

The ensign laughed. "Yes, sir. Whatever, sir. Hasn't been a war in my lifetime."

"Nor mine. Why are you smiling at me? We've met before, haven't we?"

"Yes, sir. When my squad came in."

"Oh, that's right. You came in on rotation."

"Yes, sir. Ensign Kirk."

Halley nodded. "I remember now. Ensign Kirk from New San Francisco by way of Hawaii."

"You do remember, sir." The ensign seemed pleased that he had made an impression on a commanding officer, even if in another branch. "You're from Chattanooga, Tennessee by way of Chattanooga, Tennessee. Never got the full story though, sir."

"By way of Brazil, ensign. But that was before we even had colonies on Mars. We might as well say by way of Ancient Mesopotamia."

"Great party town, Chattanooga, sir. Happening metropolis. Never been but hear about it all the time."

"It is a great town."

"But why do you say Mesopotamia, sir?"

"Can't say Africa or Asia. That would be a cop-out. Those are continents. You got to pick a place.

Mesopotamia. One of the earliest known regions of human civilization. Known for the invention of the wheel and the beginnings of mathematics and astronomy. No Mesopotamia. No Lieutenant Halley and Ensign Kirk talking aboard the NCS Neil deGrasse Tyson on the way to Titan."

"True, sir," Kirk said with a grin. "Anything to report, sir, about the trip?"

"Smooth space sailing all the way, ensign."

The ensign was satisfied. "Where are we taking you, sir?"

"C and C. Can't keep the skipper waiting, ensign."

"Yes, sir."

The young ensign was like any other new officer aboard the Tyson. Most of the Tyson's crew of scientists and soldiers had been stationed aboard for years. But with the Titan project now less than a year away—a century in the making—the cruiser's standard four-hundred-person crew would be increased to its max of five hundred with new military and tech personnel. The young soldier was excited and overwhelmed at the same time at his new historic post. Halley knew if the new ensign fell into the rotation for his first tour of duty at this late date to serve aboard the Tyson, it meant he was truly among the best. All of the officers had arrived on the Tyson not too long ago aboard a similar Dolphin-class shuttle. With the Titan mission so close, there would be only new staff arriving—scientists, soldiers, techs, and architects.

Halley was happy to see that Earth training had not been slack. The ensign was a natural. The casual chat was anything but and all part of his duties. His instructors had drilled into him, and every other soldier, sailor, and Marine, that the two greatest threats in space were radiation and space madness. How many actual reported cases were there of someone going "mental"? He knew of none and had never met any in the Army who did. But in space, "Safe Not Sorry" was the accepted mantra and promoted by all. Help of any kind was weeks or months away, or even longer the farther away they traveled. Loss of structural integrity of a ship could mean the death of everyone aboard. This fact was at the back of every crew member's mind at all times, which was why everyone kept their zero-belt on at all times—asleep, shower, toilet. Space exploration was amazing but inherently dangerous. The ship's sensors scanned new arrivals thoroughly for any physical, electromagnetic, or biological anomalies. But as a line officer, the ensign would scan the lieutenant and all his gear again with a hand scanner, and then another arriving ensign would scan again. While the scanning and intake occurred, other staff watched from secure rooms.

"What's your name, ensign?" Halley asked of the other Navy spaceman.

"Doppler, sir."

Kirk was clearly the senior of the two junior officers. He continued the small talk as he led Halley to the elevators. Doppler followed. The casual conversation was of the highest importance. The intake chat was a verbal assessment of a new arrival or returnee. He was looking for slurred speech or slow speech, lack of comprehension, wild eyes, or odd behavior of any kind.

The elevator opened and two armed Navy spacemen—one male, one female—waited in the lift. Kirk reached for the palm pad in one of the armed sailor's hands and tapped the display. Halley saw his own name and photo on the display. Kirk had cleared his boarding.

"Thanks, ensign," Halley said.

"See you in the mess, sir." Kirk looked at the other sailors. "C and C."

Kirk and Doppler stepped out of the lift and Halley carried in his gear. The door closed and lights flashed on the wall as it moved horizontally. No conversation here.

Lieutenant "Star Boy's" sour face greeted him as soon as the elevator door opened. Lieutenant Carl Centaurus, known as "Star Boy" before his promotion, stepped back to allow Halley to exit the lift with his gear.

"Thanks, sailors," Halley said to the two Navy spacemen.

"Have a good day, sir," one of them replied.

Halley stepped out.

"Need a hand?" Lieutenant Carl Centaurus asked. But he didn't wait. He grabbed the duffel bag from Halley's hand and slung it onto his shoulder.

Centaurus was about Halley's height and weight but always looked like he spent all his time on a tanning bed.

"Why do I have the honor of a personal greeting by Lieutenant Star Boy?" Halley asked.

"You know I hate that name."

"I hate mine too but you don't pick your own nickname. At least yours makes sense."

"Yours makes more sense for those of us in the know."

"What do you need, Carl? I can carry my gear to my own quarters."

"I need to talk to you."

Halley sighed. "Sure."

Once the door opened after an automated palm and retinal scan, Halley led his fellow officer into his quarters. Crew quarters aboard any cosmoship were small but not cramped. Officers had double the space of enlisted or civilians but it was no spacious Terran abode. Quarters were designed for safety, not comfort, though the Company made sure to add the niceties too. One side of the room was the sleeping quarters—more like an escape capsule pretending to be a bunk bed. Adjacent was the sitting area, which gave the occupant some freedom of choice—lounge area for entertainment, home office with desk, or both. Opposite the main door was the door to the head, or, as some military called it, a closet pretending to be a lavatory and shower. Next to it was an area most often used by residents for storage lockers. Everything in the room was stored away or fastened down at all times, so in the event of a catastrophic impact, one wouldn't be killed by flying projectiles like a lamp, brush, or pen. No kitchenettes in a room, but everyone had small refrigeration units. The layout of the living quarters was the same throughout the ship.

Halley threw the duffel bag from his shoulder onto his bed, then grabbed the one from Centaurus. "What's up, Carl?"

"You know what's up. Why would you do this to me?"

"Do what?"

"You know what. Why are you allowing me to be promoted over you?"

Halley did a double-take. "How do you know that?"

"Josh, you're not the only one who knows people in Command. What did you imagine would happen with me being promoted to captain and Army commanding officer over you when everyone knows you're next in line?"

"I don't want to be captain."

"What does that mean?"

"They're fast-tracking me."

"And?"

"If I get fast-tracked too fast, they'll bounce me off the Tyson mission. The whole reason I became an officer from enlisted and jumped through all the hoops in the service was to get here."

"Josh, I understand what you're saying but think of what it'll do to me. You'll undermine me in the eyes of the crew."

"I'll be your first officer."

"That's bull and you know it. How can you be my first officer when you have far more experience than I do? Josh, I'm not going to let you screw me like this. Find another way."

"They plan to promote me to captain, then bounce me out and to major. Then bye-bye Titan."

"They wouldn't do that to you."

"Yes, they would. Warlock has been griping about not having a major to report to him for forever. They have their laser eyes locked on me. I'm not going to have them bounce me off the mission."

"I say you have a heart-to-heart with Warlock. That should be your move."

Halley looked at him for a bit.

"You did already."

"I did."

"When?"

"Last week. Why do you think I'm late getting back and came in by myself on some stray shuttle? I tried to go above him."

"Above him? Go above an admiral. That qualifies as either space madness or super big titanium balls."

"Carl, I'm not happy."

"Figure it out. But figure it out without screwing me over. You're the captain and Army commanding officer. Don't you know the squad already has your promotion surprise party ready to go?"

"What?"

"Yes. Josh, they couldn't have you as acting captain forever. Navy has a captain. Army has to have a captain. Parity at all times. You know this."

Halley sighed again. He looked around at his neat, tidy, spartan quarters. He sat on his bed.

"Did we get final orders yet?"

"Not yet. But any day now."

"Any new crew?"

"Just the new rotations from two weeks ago."

"Yeah, one of them checked me in."

"There are discussions about having the Marines join us."

"What?"

"Yes, the scientists are up in arms. You're going to get an earful. 'We're colonizing Titan, not invading it!'"

"Is that your impersonation of Good News Girl?"

"Did it fool you?"

"Needs work."

"So, are you putting on your rank, captain?" Halley said nothing. "I know. Talk to Good News Girl. She's a high IQ scientist. She's bound to have a plan."

"I'm high IQ, too."

"Need high IQ from another branch. They think differently."

"They think scientist. We think soldier."

"But if the Command puppet masters have a plan for you, that supersedes any plan we come up with. Still, I'll think of something. I'd better check in with the skipper before she sends armed sailors for me."

"Or announces your name over the P.A. 'Captain Halley, please report to C and C."

Halley jumped to his feet. "That I don't want her to do."

The two men walked to the door. Halley stopped and reached out his hand to Centaurus. Carl's face showed the worry he was still feeling. He tentatively shook Josh's hand.

"I'm not going to undermine you, Carl. We have a good team here."

"I know."

"And I'm not going to mess it up. Have command staff ready to meet when I get out of there."

"Yes, sir."

The men exited and Halley stopped as soon as he closed the door. "But no surprise promotion parties."

"Not sure I can stop them."

"Well, I have full confidence in my exec officer's abilities to do so."

"Yes, sir."

Scientists wanting to be among the stars entered the Navy to "sail the seas of space"; soldiers went into the Army. A partnership naturally coalesced to become Military Science, or Mil-Sci. To explore space, the scientists needed the military, while the military needed the scientists for a renewed raison d'être in space defense. The coming era of terraforming would be a boon to both. Generations ago, advanced drone technology, energy freedom, better and more stable governments around the globe, and the rarity of war on the planet were decimating both science and military services to near extinction. So, they joined forces to re-imagine and rebrand themselves to multinationals and world governments.

Once, there had been eight different branches of the military. Today, there were three: Navy, Army, and Marines. But Mil-Sci was the union of the Navy and Army. The "barbarians" (the Marines) were called in for the real violence when it was needed.

The Army-Navy partnership had always been, and remained, an uneasy one. The scientists of the Navy saw the Tyson as a space-faring, floating city for advanced science. Army soldiers viewed it as the military's flagship in space. The key to the alliance, as Planet Tamers MN rightly ascertained ages ago, was the leadership—a Navy commanding officer not afraid to be a soldier when needed and an Army commanding officer who could understand what the scientists were saying from moment to moment. In Planet Tamers, Human Resources had the best psychologists and profilers. Only two people were the foundation for an entire ship's operations, effectiveness, morale, success, and...profits. Planet Tamers spent the time and resources to ensure they got it right.

The tethered forward navigation and operations

section was known as Command and Control, or simply C and C. Navy called it the brain of the cosmoship; Army called it the heart and soul of the ship.

Halley exited the lift at the neck of the ship to waiting security. He'd be scanned and checked before being given entrance to the sensitive area. It was one of the few areas of the ship where the scientists welcomed, and demanded, armed Army soldiers. The privates carried standard-issue green-camouflaged rifles.

"Welcome back, sir," one of the enlisted soldiers said to him.

"Thank you, private. Good to be back. Anything to report?"

"Nothing of note, sir. Everyone's just excited to finally get to the Titan and start terraforming already."

"Copy that in the strongest terms, private."

"Sir, is it true that since we'll be the first colonists, we get dibs on the land we terraform?" asked another soldier.

"Private, we're not the colonists. We're the conquerors. After us, will be the builders. Last will come the colonists."

"Conquerors, sir?"

"Forget the political correctness. We need to conquer the environment first for everyone to be able to do what they need to do. What did you think I meant by 'conquer'? No one lives on Titan so we don't have to worry about little green extraterrestrials. We'll clean it all up and make it look nice so that when our military and corporate bosses arrive with the media and step onto Titan soil, their feet won't get dirty."

"Clean-up crew? Sir, I think you've managed to thoroughly depress us."

"Don't worry. That emotion won't last long. You'll be too busy with work for any emotions."

"Will we even be allowed to shoot an ET, sir?"

"Sure, private, I'll put the Halloween costume on you myself and tell the Sarge to spare no bullets when we send you running along Titan terrain butt naked."

The four enlisted on duty broke out in laughter.

"Buzz me in, private," he said to the corporal.

A glass door slid open and closed behind Halley as he walked up metal stairs. He was now the only green-fatigued Army personnel (soldier) to be seen. In space, the scientists wore navy blue fatigues, not white lab coats. The color pattern of the forward section was like a lab—spotless white everything: walls, ceilings, and walls. Too sterile for Halley's liking but that was how it had always been. He preferred the darker mauves, maroons, plums, and beiges of the rest of the ship and its living quarters.

Halley glanced at his timepiece, a cream-colored band around his right wrist. Change of watch was happening. The Tyson, like most Company ships, was on six-hour watch cycles. New shifts were coming on and the old shifts were leaving for the mess or their quarters. He recognized most of the personnel as they passed him in the halls.

The doors to the Control Room opened and a woman came out—the Skipper's Executive Officer, Commander Cassiopeia.

"Commander," he greeted.

"Lieutenant," she replied as they passed each other.

Inside the Control Room, the design always reminded him of an Earth aquatic passenger cruise ship.   All the stations faced the main front observation window. Command was dead center, about ten feet back, with

Helm to the left and Tactical to the right. Sensors (or "Eyes") were to the far left and the Watch station was to the far right both between Command and the observation.

Captain Ayla was on her feet, waiting next to the command chair. She turned around to see Halley enter. He noticed her eyes squinting, as she was looking not at his face but below his eye-line.

"Why am I not calling you captain, Lieutenant?" she asked in her typical dry way.

"Checking in, skipper," he said.

"Ignoring the question. Took you long enough to get here, Lieutenant. You can walk with me to the mess."

Officers were on duty at all the stations except one.

"Are you missing someone?"

"My commander will be back. I actually sent her on an errand related to you. Hence my question."

Halley followed Ayla out of the Control Room and back into the hall. "I'll tell you what I told my X.O.: no premature surprise parties."

"Is it premature? Or is there something you want to share with me? I know you Army types aren't as efficient as the Navy but even your branch can't be that slow in making official what you've already been doing for more than two years."

"A year."

"Much more than a year."

"It's in the works."

"Now I know something's up."

"Oh, I heard the Marines are coming."

"Let's step into my boudoir," Ayla said as she led him into the captain's private mess. Halley had his own private dining room too, though he never used it, preferring to eat with his crew. Ayla was the opposite.

"Does your juvenile attempt at changing the subject actually work with real people?" she asked as she led him to the table to sit down.

"I find I'm most successful with Navy types."

"Probably Marines."

"Them, too."

"Why aren't you a captain, Lieutenant? I thought that's why you made your day trip. We have an unequal balance aboard my ship. That will not do. We need two captains, not one."

"I know that."

"Then in taking full advantage of senior rank, I want it sorted by oh-eight-hundred. No delay. We'll get our final mission orders any day now and—"

"We haven't received them yet? You should have gotten them no later than yesterday."

"Whenever the final orders come in, they will be read by the Tyson's commanding officers of the rank of captain and above. I'm not joking, Halley."

"Let me ask you something."

"Oh, no. Whenever you start a sentence with that phrase, it means something bad or unpleasant."

"That's not true."

"It is."

"What about Centaurus as—"

Ayla jumped up from her seat as if she had been electro-shocked. The stern look on her face was real anger.

The door to the mess opened and an ensign came in with two trays. The junior officer stopped for a moment, wondering what she had walked into.

"Set them down, ensign, and go about your day."

"Yes, ma'am."

The ensign placed one still smoking hot tray of food in front of Halley and the other where the captain was sitting.

"Thank the chef for me, ensign," Ayla said. "Bye-bye."

"Welcome, ma'am." The ensign left the room.

Ayla sat down and folded her arms, looking at Halley.

"Why would I want that knuckle-dragger as the Army commanding officer of my ship?"

"That is unfair."

"A grown man with the name of Star Boy."

"That's just his call sign and also unfair. Carl is a solid officer."

"What happened to Joshua?"

"Nothing happened to me."

"Is Carl part of this?"

"Part of what? No."

"Did you speak with him about it?"

"We discussed it this morning."

"We? You haven't been on board long enough to discuss anything with anybody. What's going on?"

"Nothing."

Halley watched as Ayla stormed out of the room. He was about to run after her but the aroma of hot food in his nostrils was too mesmerizing. He hadn't had real, hot food in days. His body wouldn't let him get up from his chair and his eyes didn't move from the white tray of food with the attached cup of the juice of the day. He picked up the fork and dug in.

The door opened. Halley turned around to see Captain Ayla with her stern look. Lieutenant Centaurus walked in and stood beside her.

"She called you names," Halley said to Centaurus.

"I'm calling you names," Ayla said. "Are you kidding me? You're sabotaging your own career. You're right. I was calling the wrong person a knuckle-dragger. What soldier sabotages their own career on purpose?"

"I'm here to be a soldier on Titan, not a glorified button-pusher on some ship off Mars or Jupiter overseeing the region for the Admiral." They both could see, in Halley's face, how upset he truly was.

"How real a possibility is this, really?" Ayla asked Centaurus.

Centaurus hesitated before he spoke. "It's real. He could get bounced. There are a lot of open slots. The last major retired last year and I can't remember when we last had a colonel. They're not going to leave the slot vacant with this operation on hand. Everything's going to be filled before we touch down on Titan."

"This is such bullshit," Ayla said. "They'd really mess up our crew to fill in names on some org chart?"

"Yes, they would," Halley said.

Ayla sat back down at the dining table and picked up her fork. "Lieutenant, you are dismissed."

A smirk came over Centaurus' face. "Glad I could be of assistance, ma'am." He turned and left the room.

"He's a solid officer, you know."

"He wouldn't be on my ship if he wasn't. Shall we have our meeting?"

"Does the Admiral know this is your ship?"

"This far away in space from the brass, I couldn't care less either way. What I care about is our orders to proceed to Titan for touchdown. But before that, squaring away out command structure situation."

Captain H.B. (Halle-Bopp) Ayla had been the Navy's commanding officer of the Tyson for ten years. Most didn't mind her calling the Tyson "her ship" because she had been aboard for close to fifteen years, rising from the rank of ensign. The only other person who came close to her years of service aboard the ship was Sarge, with eighteen years, but those years were nonconsecutive.

The captain and gifted scientist also had the military call sign of Good News Girl, which in her case was meant to be the opposite of her personality. However, Halley had always gotten along with her fine. There was no tension between Army and Navy on the Tyson, which was another reason why the post was so sought after. Halley joined the crew only three years ago but had completely changed the spirit of the place for the better. His predecessors were hotshots who cared very little about the science mission of the ship and very much about maintaining separation between the branches. All that went away when Halley took over. In fact, it was the real reason Ayla didn't care for Centaurus. Carl was from the previous regime and Halley had been brought in over him.

The meal was done and Halley reviewed the reports on his tablet. Ayla viewed the same reports on hers.

"Why won't anyone tell me where your nickname Bogeyman comes from?" Ayla asked.

Halley looked up from his screen. "What? Where did that come from?"

Ayla said nothing, keeping her eyes on her tablet screen.

"If you haven't sweated it out of my soldiers after three years, you should stop trying. Besides, I hate my nickname with the subdued rage and intensity of the sun."

"Join the club."

Reports were the bane of any officer in command. There was always someone above you wanting a report on something. Halley knew his feelings were no different from those of every other C.O. in the history of the military. He spent more time gathering and compiling reports than he did exercising, practicing at the firing range, eating, or engaging in any other activity. It never ended. At least he had a fellow C.O. to commiserate with on a regular basis.

He finished reading the captain's logs filed during his absence. Ayla's was so thorough that he was confident he now knew anything there was to know. Then to the department reports.

"How many new crew members did you get?" he asked.

"We're at full strength. Morale officer, rec officer, PX officers, transportation officer, legal officer, chaplain. But the only ones I care about are my two xenometeorologists."

"How many weather people do you need?"

"Methane rain, Hadley vortexes, cryo-volcanoes. When we touch down on Titan, you'll say we don't have enough. How many new soldiers did you get?"

"One squad so far. Command is readying a full company. What about these Marines?"

"I was told a platoon of them will rendezvous with us there."

"We don't have the room."

"We are to make room."

"Why? That's why I'm here. My soldiers can handle any trouble. Unless—"

"Unless there's some other trouble we don't know about."

"What aren't they telling us?"

"The salient question."

"I'll make some calls too and see if I can find anything."

"Please do. I don't want Marines on my ship. They're noisy and there's not enough room on the ship to accommodate all the stupid weapons and bombs and robots they carry everywhere they go."

"Before we go calling them stupid, let's find out if there's some trouble we don't know about. If there is, I'm happy to let them—and not my soldiers—fight it."

"Agreed."

"What about your Navy fighting?"

"My scientists are lovers, not fighters. That's your gig."

Halley chuckled.

The department reports were equally thorough, routine, and boring: Ops, Engineering, Weapons, Supplies, and Medical.

"We should accelerate the touchdown drills for the crew," Ayla said.

"We don't want to burn them out. Why not throw in some terraforming drills for fun?"

"Fun?"

"Yes, you've heard of it."

"I don't partake in it myself but I have heard it can be useful. Terraforming isn't supposed to be fun."

"Ayla, it's a drill. Break up the monotony of the endless drills that your crew and mine have been at for over a year and can do in their sleep. Variety is a proven scientific technique to keep humans engaged and productive. Yes?"

"Yes. Agreed. Terraforming drills it is. Even though

the actual terraforming could be many months away."

"Ayla, fun. The watchword is fun."

"Okay, okay. Terraforming drills."

Halley had designed the drills himself. The reality was that neither Army nor Navy would do the actual terraforming. The terraforming of a new planetary body was highly specialized and highly classified. Planet Tamers called the actual personnel "genesis architects" and they would arrive only after the Tyson crew landed on Titan, surveyed the land, chose the site for the first settlement, prepared the site, and put in place all the land, air, and orbital security. What exactly the genesis architects did was subject to wild speculation and rumors among the general scientific, military, and civilian communities. The Planet Tamers board of directors said the process was "magical." The reclusive chairman of the board went further and said that the work of genesis architects ultimately transforming a planetary body to be habitable by plant, animal, and human life as "god-like." Or it could all be PR "bullshit," according to Good News Girl.

"May I say that you are very atypical for a scientist," Halley commented, still reading a report on the tablet.

"A good scientist is supposed to be skeptical of all

things."

"Skepticism isn't the problem. You don't seem to have enough of the child-like wonder of science, which, to be frank, I have, and I'm a soldier. A favorite quote for us space explorers: 'Rockets didn't take us to the moon; it was the engineers and the dreamers.'"

"Goodness. Halley's reciting inspirational quotes. Don't let your crew hear you talk like this. They'll think we cloned and replaced you with an impostor. Okay, I admit, I'm a bit inspired for the moment."

"Then let's savor the moment."

"Savored and moving on." She looked up from her tablet. "But are we doing any of this for altruistic reasons? Truly. Why are we doing this?"

"Strange questions for a scientist to ask, especially one living on a space research and exploration ship for most of her adult life."

"I always question my existence and motives. I wish more people did the same. This Earth movement to terraform a planet—I know why I want to do it. But why does everyone else? Why do you?"

"Honestly, because it's there. It's really that simple for me. We already have a planet. Now we want a second one. It's a big 'whatever' to me. If it gives humanity, and this soldier, something to do, terraforming planets rather than wars, I couldn't be happier. What else am I going to do with my existence? That's all the philosophizing from me this week."

"Inspirational quotes and Socratic philosophy all in the same day. You should leave and come back more often if that's all it takes to boost a soldier's IQ."

"But you didn't answer my question."

"Was there a question?"

"You already have the high IQ, so you know the question."

"You won't answer mine."

"Why my nickname is Bogeyman will be for next time. If I give you the book and tell you the ending, you won't read the book. I want you to read the book."

Ayala smiled. "What's wrong with you today? Quotes, philosophy, analogies. Now I'm getting scared you really are an imposter. Tin soldiers don't talk like this."

"Yes, we do. So, tell this tin soldier why such a committed skeptic is at the forefront of what will be the most historic operation ever in human history.

Operation Fairy Dancer. The terraforming of Titan. You're going to be part of history yourself. The kiddies are going to be taught about you in class."

"You too."

"Maybe. Captains, at least on the soldiering side, normally don't make it into the history books. Scientists, it's different. For us, you have to get to at least general. Don't like admirals, though."

"Don't tell Warlock that."

"Well?"

"Ironically, when space exploration was motivated by the war effort, it was probably at its most pure. Are we doing all this to truly explore space and better humankind? Or are we only bettering the bank accounts of the multinationals of Earth, or worse, are we pawns in some trillionaire's hobby because they're bored?

"Why didn't we do all this before? Because there's no money in space exploration. But space mining. A gold mine. Mining every asteroid, rock, and moon they can find. Eventually, it will end, and we humans get bored so easily. Suddenly, space colonizing came back into vogue and so did that word: terraforming. Notice we don't want to terraform Mars. It's closer and easier, right? Mars would be perfect. Terraform the Red Planet, then move on. But that's not glamorous enough. No, we start with faraway Titan. A bigger payday for a multinational. Terraform Mars and profits for a few decades at most. Terraform another planet or moon—like Europa or Enceladus or better, Titan. Insane profits for a century or more. Planet Tamers is going to be a real estate company. You and I are its location scouts, surveyors, and low-end construction crew."

"Very cynical, you are. All that may be true but none of it matters. It's not why you became a scientist and why you're here now."

"My reason isn't much different from yours. I was a little girl, looked up at the stars one night, and heard them calling my name. The Call of the Stars. I knew my life would have to do with getting closer to them in some way. I'm here today because humanity will always advance despite itself. Today, we have Terrans. Tomorrow, we'll have Terrans and Titans. And I'll be part of that new frontier despite the multinationals and their latest klepto-capitalistic schemes. Humanity will advance."

"I say someone has to pay the bill."

"Someone does. Sadly, the true philanthropists for

science died out a long time ago. Only governments or capitalists can write the big check. So, I gladly accept the big check and pretend to do what they want me to do as I maintain the nobility of science—and, if I'm lucky, get a slew of awards and a nice statue in posthumous honor."

"There. That wasn't so hard to answer."

Ayla pointed at him. "I'll hold you to your promise, Captain Bogeyman. I'll know your call sign's origin before we reach Titan."

Strangely, there were few places for large meetings on the Tyson. If Army wanted a place, there was the mess hall, but that was shared with Navy. There were the science labs but Army was restricted unless accompanied by Navy personnel. The engine rooms were restricted to everyone not on the technical teams. Command didn't want anyone near the Helios engines if those individuals were not directly responsible for their upkeep. Halley found the perfect spot away from Navy and ship surveillance—the Army's own shuttle bay, and inside one of their own three craft. They had two Dolphin-class shuttles and one Narwhal-class defender craft.

Their defender ship was big enough for a full platoon with all its weapons and gear. Techs kept it spotless and in tip-top readiness but in all the years it sat in bay, it had never been used. That was, except for Halley's meetings in the three years he'd been their acting commanding office.

"Quiet down, primates!" Staff Sergeant "God of War" Ogun yelled at the assembled men. He looked at the X.O. "Am I doing your job again, sir?"

The soldiers laughed as Lieutenant Centaurus shook his head. "Sarge, nobody can scream like you can. At least, that's what the ladies tell me."

Assembled were Corporal "Crack Shot" Yuri, PFC "Leo the Lion" Zapata, and the huge PFC "Minotaur" Balkan. The Tyson had almost two hundred soldiers aboard—equivalent to the Navy's numbers—but these six men of one officer and five enlisted made up Halley's command staff—something else he had put in place when he came in as Army commanding officer.

"Sir, I don't think you're quite dressed," PFC Zapata called out from his position sprawled on the seats along the wall of the main compartment of the craft. His fellow soldiers were seated next to him or across.

"What do you mean, private?" Halley asked, standing in front of them.

"Yeah, aren't you missing some rank on that shoulder of yours, sir?" Corporal Yuri asked.

Halley glanced at a grinning Centaurus. "My men, my wonderful men."

"Sir, I bumped into those Navy types and they got females all over the place," PFC Zapata began. "Where are the women for our command staff?"

"Private, you are not command," Lieutenant Centaurus interjected.

"Okay, men, as far as women on the 'command team' are concerned, I told you once, I told you a hundred times, that's your job. Not mine. You're the 'command team.' We got two hundred soldiers on this floating sardine can. I'll promote male, female, or vegetable if they can pass all the tests and drills you did. I think it's funny. Army can't find females for its command. Navy can't find men for theirs."

"They got one guy," Corporal Yuri said.

"He doesn't count," PFC Zapata said. "He's the brother of one of the females. I smell unfair advantage."

"Are they twins?" Sarge asked. "Twins don't have to look like each other."

"Fraternal twins, Sarge. That's the word you're searching for, as opposed to identical twins." PFC Zapata smiled from ear to ear. "I'm smart and know stuff." He looked at Yuri. "They got one guy on their 'command team.'"

Yuri nodded and made loud sniffing sounds. "I smell naked, sweaty, nepotism."

"As for my pending promotion," Halley said. All the men got quiet and sat up. "It will happen when it happens. Regardless, I'm the C.O. and, more importantly, I'm already getting the pay adjustment."

The men broke out in applause. That satisfied them.

"I assembled our quick pow-wow to reflect on the momentous events that we all will be in the middle of in a few short months. The L.T., the Sarge, and I have been waiting years for this. You new soldiers were in school but I'm sure you were waiting then, too. Probably enlisted so you could be a part of it. Reminds me of a quote, since I'm looking at PFC Yuri's ugly face. "The men laughed. 'I see Earth! It is so beautiful.' That gem was from Yuri Gagarin, Earth's first human in space."

"Sir, not to interrupt you," Corporal Yuri said with his hand raised.

"Go ahead and interrupt me since you already did."

"I appreciate it and I'm flattered but it's not going to work, sir," Yuri said.

"What are you talking about, corporal?"

"You're going for something like 'The Poet' or 'Aristotle' or 'Socrates,' right, sir?"

"I have no idea what you're talking about, corporal."

"Once you get your nickname, sir, it's for life. You're Bogeyman and that's all there is to it. You can throw around quotes until we get to the Andromeda galaxy."

"Corporal, I appreciate the words. Really, I do. I really appreciate the suggestions, too. Never thought of The Poet. Actually, I like it. So Bogeyman says: The Poet it is. X.O., Sarge. It's settled."

"Cap, what's the rest of your quote story before we all forget?" Sarge asked.

"Oh, yes. 'I see Earth! It is so beautiful.' From Yuri Gagarin. The mission to turn Saturn's largest moon, Titan, into Earth Two is within Army spitting distance. When the first phase is complete, the media will report it across the solar system as they quote me verbatim: 'I see New Titan! It is so beautiful.' People will ask what fine captain said that and the media will say, The Poet."

"Didn't see that one coming," PFC Balkan said.

"Caught me completely by surprise," Corporal Yuri said.

"Never would have guessed that ending, sir," PFC Zapata said.

Sarge looked at Lieutenant Centaurus. "Sir, do you think the men are actually laughing in alternative realities in the multiverse?"

Chapter Two

The Call

M aking the rounds of the Tyson was not part of his official duties, but Halley did it anyway. From stem to stern, he physically walked every part of the cosmoship and visited every department, Army and Navy. His Army predecessors had never ventured into Navy areas of the ship, and technically it wasn't operating procedure, but Halley didn't do it out of some misguided quirk. He did it so that every soldier and sailor aboard would see his face on at least a weekly basis. Navy personnel had been suspicious of his visits at first but three years later expected them.

Halley walked into the science labs. The Navy's pride and joy were spacious and always busy.

"Army spy on deck," one scientist called out to laughs.

"Hide all documents revealing Navy's plot to subjugate all Army and Marine forces and take over Earth," another said.

"Who said scientists, even Navy ones, can't crack jokes?" Halley said as he casually walked through the lab. He noticed two of Ayla's senior scientists: Ensigns Rosen-bridge and Kirkwood, the brother-sister team.

"Ensign," he said to Rosen-bridge who always seemed to be doing experiments with flasks and Petri dishes around, her eyes glued to a microscope.

She looked up. "Lieutenant."

He always felt nervous around a scientist whose call sign was "Symbiote."

"Sir, when are you going to let me make you dinner?"

"Ensign, I'd say, like, never."

He reached Ensign Kirkwood.

"Lieutenant, I got something that you might find interesting," the scientist said with boyish exuberance, leading Halley to a cylindrical glass case. The bottom half was filled with brown sand. The sand moved.

"What's that?"

"Sir, this is going to be my contribution to the terraforming project. Genetically engineered worms."

"Worms?"

"We'll introduce them to the Titan site. A few hundred of them after we create the proper cordoned-off section."

"We're going to Titan and you're going to dump worms there. I don't think Saturn will like us Earthers dumping worms on its moon."

"No, they're not common worms. Titan's surface is mainly frozen water ice, hydrocarbons, ammonia ice from its volcanoes. Our friends here will burrow into the ground, eating as they go, and excrete a highly-rich nutrient loam."

"Loam?"

"The best blend for plant growth is called loam. Black dirt. Earth's optimum mixture of sand, clay, and silt for the best crops. Holds in the nutrients and water but drains effectively and allows oxygen infiltration."

"Excretions?"

"Yes, sir."

"Shit?"

"Good shit, sir."

Halley shook his head and then looked back at Kirkwood's sister. "Your parents had to lock the two of you in the basement, didn't they?"

"Who do you think taught us all this, sir?" Kirkwood said.

"We loved the basement," Rosen-bridge said. "We did all our experiments there. Loved it. So did our parents."

"Just keep your worms on the Navy side."

Halley was in the sick bay talking to Medical Officer McAuliffe when the door opened and Commander Cassiopeia came in. The sick bay, like most Navy sections, was spacious with lots of white surfaces. The room had a dozen bio-beds in the main foyer, a doctor's office and consulting room, and its own medical lab with a small staff.

"Hello, Lieutenant," Commander Cassiopeia said to Halley.

"Commander," he replied.

"You have a priority call from Command waiting in your quarters."

That got Halley's attention. "Priority." He turned to Dr. McAuliffe. "Thanks for the info, Doctor."

"Always a pleasure, Army."

Halley double-timed out of the sick bay. The commander followed.

"You could have simply called me on my comm," Halley said to her. "Aren't you on duty?"

"I'm touched by your diligence in Navy operations. I was making my own rounds. Maybe it's about your rank."

"Hardly a priority call. But I'd better find out what. Do you know who's holding?"

"The Admiral himself."

"Why didn't you say that before?"

Halley bolted from her, racing down the hall.

Halley got to his quarters and sat at his desk, then touched the flashing button.

"Admiral," Halley greeted. "You didn't need to hold. I would have called you right back."

"No, it's okay, Josh."

In the military, when a high-ranking senior officer called you by your first name, it was a bad omen. Admiral "Warlock" Antarus' face was sullen. Something was wrong.

"Yes, Admiral?"

Admiral Zed Antarus was at the top of the food chain for every soldier, sailor, and Marine in deep space. He was the boss of everyone's boss out there. At his level, both officer and enlisted could go their entire career and never hear from him once. Halley had now seen the man twice, face-to-face by way of view screen, in so many days. The first time was unusual but logical. This second time knocked the wind out of the lieutenant.

"We lost contact with Uroboros."

Halley closed his eyes and rubbed his forehead over and over. "Admiral, you wouldn't be calling me directly if you simply lost contact with Uroboros."

"Anything I say will be nothing more than

speculation. The facts as we know them are that no one is aboard the space station."

"Bodies?"

"None have been sighted aboard that are visible from satellite and nothing floating in space."

"What's the speculation, sir?"

"Catastrophic event of a natural or man-made order."

"Man-made? What does that mean, sir? Were they attacked?"

"We don't know. But there does seem to be some damage to the space station."

"Admiral, why are we talking? Send in a team from Mars. It's right there."

"Lieutenant, I'm going to say something to you but you do not have the authorization to disclose this to anyone else—not your X.O., Navy, doctor, or chaplain. We do not have any teams on Mars, and we cannot let anyone know that Uroboros is in trouble. To that end, the NCS Konstantin Rokossovsky is on its way."

"What?"

"It's on its way as we speak."

"Admiral, my father is on that space station."

"Which is why I'm calling."

"I thought you were calling to have me lead the team there."

"No. I owe you this call."

"Why did you do this, Admiral? You should never have told me. What do you think I'm going to do? You're telling me the whole crew, including my father is missing. You can't send in a team from Mars because there's no Earth Alliance team on Mars. That you can't tell the Martian civilians. You're sending in a war cruiser that will take a year to get there even at maximum burn. Why did you call me and ruin my day, Admiral? I'm effectively less than useless to my men, the Army, and the Tyson. There's no way I'm sitting on the Tyson waiting for you to get to Uroboros. I bet this brilliance was your bosses' brilliance. Those five-stars on Earth, were they ever real soldiers, sailors, or Marines, sir? Does close proximity to political a-hole leaders destroy their brain cells, make them forgot what it's like to be a soldier, to be a man, to be a human being? This is why we call them brain-deads and knee-pad wearers and sycophantic, supercilious, sell-outs behind their backs. I'm sitting here on Tyson while my father could be dying somewhere. Maybe he's dead already and his body is floating in space. So what? He's a human being. His body deserves to be buried like that of every other decent Earther. That's the Army way. And if you don't mind me saying, Admiral, that's the Navy way, too. The Marine way too. No one left behind! Even scientists. Even civilians. I'm not staying here in my quarters. I'm going to march out of here, put together a plan, and go to the Belt if I have to, by myself. I can do it, and you know I can. You know why my call sign is Bogeyman. You're sending the NCS Konstantin Rokossovsky. It's not even at Mars. What a massive load of crap! One year away. 'Catastrophic event of a natural or man-made order.' Natural is meteors and you would have said so. You're saying the station was attacked! I'm not staying here. I can get started for the Uroboros now."

Halley held in his growing rage and despair. He waited for the tirade of anger and curses to spew forth from the Admiral's mouth. However, the Admiral's nonchalant expression never changed

"Lieutenant Halley, your request for leave is approved."

Chapter Three

Departure

Inside the Control Room, the bridge officers watched the shuttle craft approach. Captain Ayla stood at Sensors manned by Ensign Sirius. She looked at her X.O. again.

"Who are they?" Captain Ayla asked.

"Entry codes are fine, ma'am," the ensign said.

"Command, this is the NCS Seahorse. Requesting permission for docking," the voice came overhead.

"Seahorse, entry code received. Permission for docking granted," Commander Cassiopeia acknowledged into her mic. She let go of the "speak" button.

"Command, received and understood. Beginning docking approach now."

Ayla walked to the conn and pressed the comm

button. "NCS Seahorse, you're not on the schedule for docking. We are on restricted status."

"Command, we have special orders from Earth Command."

"Orders?"

"Yes, command. Special orders to deliver directly."

"Understood, Seahorse."

Ayla glanced at her commander.

"We were wondering why we hadn't gotten them yet," Commander Cassiopeia said.

"Maybe so but this isn't procedure."

"Our mission is far from procedure anymore, ma'am. We'll be creating new procedures and rule books as we go."

Ayla watched all the monitors closely as the shuttle made contact. The ship looked like a Dolphin-class military shuttle, the favorite of the work-horse for transporting squads and small cargo loads. From the monitor outside the docking bay, she saw the receiving crew approach. She pushed a comm button. "Ensigns, hold on. Call Army and have them send some soldiers to back you up."

"Ma'am?" Ensign Kirk said into his shoulder comm.

"You heard me, ensign. Keep their bay door closed until they arrive. We have to give Army something to do besides sleep all day."

"Yes, ma'am."

"Command, is there a problem? Bay door hasn't opened."

Ayla touched another comm button. "Stand by, Seahorse. Doors opening soon."

"Acknowledged, command."

The ensign on Sensors noticed something. "Ma'am, they've stopped their power down cycle."

Captain Ayla and Commander Cassiopeia looked at each other.

"Why would they do that?" Captain Ayla said. She touched the comm button. "Seahorse, please power down. You're making us nervous up here."

"They're powered up, ma'am," the ensign called out.

Captain Ayla hit an emergency button and the barrier doors closed fast, startling the docking bay receiving crew.

From another monitor, they saw the shuttle suddenly pull away, ripping its seal. The bridge could hear men scream but they were safe. Containment held with the emergency barriers in place. However, the bridge was shocked as they watched the shuttle race away from the Tyson.

"Weapons, battle stations. Weapons?" Ayla yelled.

The ensign at Tactical hit button after button by instinct but her expression was one of complete panic. "Battle stations activated, ma'am."

"Activate all rail guns."

"Rail guns activated. No lock, ma'am."

"Watch, damage report?" Ayla asked.

"No structural damage. No hull damage, ma'am," said the ensign at Watch station.

"Sensors, where are they?" Ayla asked.

"Tracking them, ma'am." The ensign went quiet. The captain and commander looked at her.

"And?" Ayla asked.

"They're gone," Commander Cassiopeia said from her station.

"Gone? Find them!" Ayla yelled.

"They must have a new stealth tech!" Commander Cassiopeia yelled.

"Red alert now!" Ayla directed.

Commander Cassiopeia hit it on her station panel.

The main door opened and Lieutenant Centaurus ran in as red lights flashed on the walls. None of them knew what triggering Red Alert looked like on the Tyson. It had never happened before.

"What's happening?" he asked.

"Where's your commanding officer, soldier?" Ayla asked him.

"He should be here, ma'am."

The door opened again and Halley walked in. Everyone stopped. No one had ever seen him look the way he did. His eyes were red as if he'd been crying. The expression on his face was one of exhaustion.

The Navy bridge crew looked at each other. He couldn't have learned what just occurred, and if he did, he wouldn't look the way he did. Halley was known as a steady hand under pressure.

"What's happening?" Halley asked. He looked at Centaurus.

"I don't know, sir. Sir, what happened to you?"

Halley closed his eyes for a moment to steady himself. "Are we under attack?"

"An unknown shuttle tried to dock. It had the correct entry codes but something wasn't right. They said they had special orders from Earth Command," Commander Cassiopeia answered.

"That's a lie. I was speaking to the Admiral," Halley said. "What happened next?"

"They docked, powered up, and ripped the air lock as they flew away."

Shocked expressions crossed the soldiers' faces.

"Everyone in the bay is okay. I activated the emergency barriers," Ayla said.

"You saved their lives," Lieutenant Centaurus said.

"I have to go," Halley said.

Not a word was spoken as they stared at him.

"My father is...the science space station in the Belt, the Uroboros was likely attacked. All hands on deck are unaccounted for. They don't know what happened and help is a year away, so I'm the rescue party or whatever I am. I'm leaving now. I'm sorry. L.T., you're commanding officer for Army while I'm gone. Sorry. You can handle all this."

Halley walked out of the Control Room.

◆ ◆ ◆

Finally, everyone snapped out of the shock of the situation. Lieutenant Centaurus was already out the door with Commander Cassiopeia following.

"Crew, stay at your stations!" Captain Ayla yelled. The commander stopped in her tracks. "I'll go after him," she said.

When she exited the Command Room, she could hear Centaurus yelling at her ensigns to know which way Halley went. But she knew, and rather than go down the steps, she turned left down the hallway.

She made good time to the Army shuttle bay and there he was. Halley was holding three duffle bags in his hands.

As he stopped at the door of one of the shuttles, he turned. "You caught me. Too bad this isn't the Navy section of the ship."

"Please, don't go. I may not understand the situation but I know the emotions."

"Your parents around?"

"They died when I was young."

"My dad is who I have left."

Ayla struggled to say something but changed her mind. "What's his name?"

"Anslem."

"Scientist or soldier?"

"One of you."

"I like him already."

"Now you have to give Centaurus a chance. Keep the Sarge close, too. He has more time in service than both of us."

"Halley, I need to see you again. You owe me that story about how you got your nickname."

"I'll be back."

"I know you hate hugs."

"I do and it's completely inappropriate in the workplace." She hugged him around all his gear.

"Keep the Tyson on course, no matter what."

"No matter what."

Ayla watched Halley board the Dolphin-class shuttle. She had so many questions. As the floor moved the shuttle to the launching area, the barriers sealed off the island. In moments, his shuttle was gone.

♦ ♦ ♦

When Captain Ayla returned to the Command Room, Lieutenant Centaurus had returned with the Sarge.

"Did you see him?" Centaurus asked.

"Yes, he's gone."

"Damn," the L.T. said.

"Sensors, where's that hostile?"

"Ma'am, nothing is showing."

"You haven't found it after all this time?" Ayla was angry. She sat in her command chair and pushed a comm button. "Sensors, what was last contact?"

"Last contact was forty-five clicks, forty-five degrees off port."

Ayla touched the comm buttons. "Seahorse, or whatever your true name is, identify yourself immediately. We have all weapons locked."

"Locked on what?" was the immediate response overhead.

The crew froze. There was no delay in the snappy response, as if the pilot had been waiting. He knew they couldn't see him, but what really unnerved them was the tone of the response. In the military, there was a protocol to communications and no one ever deviated from it. The person speaking to them was not military, or any that they had ever encountered. Ayla could see the fear in the faces of her crew members, as she knew they could see it in her face.

"Do you know what your ship looks like from here? It's like a goose. Long neck. Long legs with an open umbrella on its feet. Which part do you want to lose first?" said the menacing voice overhead.

Ayla rose from her chair. She stared at the ensign on Sensors. The junior officer was almost in tears as she shook her head.

"Unidentified vessel, you are to move out of weapons range immediately." The voice belonged to Halley! "Be advised that this is your only warning. You have three seconds to comply."

"Shut up!" the hostile yelled.

"You first," Halley said.

The Commander jumped up from her chair, staring at her monitors. She slapped a button and the image appeared on the main view screen. The enemy shuttle was just off their starboard, exploding in a flash of light. Then all that was left was floating debris, which they could now hear crashing against the hull.

They stared at each other with their mouths wide open.

"Tyson, threat is neutralized. I'll see you when I see you, on Titan." Halley's voice cut out and that was that.

Chapter Four

The Uju Kauboi

Music of any kind was prohibited in the cockpit. Military pilots had to keep their ears attuned to every minute sound around them. Even the smallest anomaly could be the beginning of a meteor shower, or God forbid, an air leak in the hull, or worse. When Halley piloted a craft, he went a step further—he amplified all the ambient sound waves hitting the craft.

As he flew away from the Tyson, his thoughts should have been on the crew. But all he focused on were the hostiles he had destroyed and the many questions that swirled around in his head. Where did they come from? A ship of its size had to have come from a larger base ship somewhere. How did they get the Tyson's approach codes? Why didn't sensors spot them when they were playing possum? What would their ultimate plans have been had they gotten aboard? Were there others?

Because of the last question, he kept all his weapons hot and maintained his propulsion on minimal burn. He set his own sensors for audible ping should any anomaly appear on the displays. For hours, that was all he did, until he was certain that he was truly alone in space. He powered up to maximum burn.

He could have taken one of the four Army star-wings—advanced military space fighters. But with the trek to Titan, and no certainty as to when he'd return, he couldn't deprive the Tyson of any part of its overall defense. Its crews would be on Titan for a long time. Some might be there for life. He'd taken one of its Dolphin-class shuttles and his super-suit. That would be all he needed.

North America had the Tyson but other countries and regions had their own cosmoship versions, known by their common civilian citizens by name and acknowledged with great national pride. The Koreans had the "Space Cowboy."

The KCS Uju Kauboi was an Argonaut-class base cruiser. It was newer but smaller than the Nautilus class. The Koreans, like most countries, had folded all their military branches into one. UROK (Unified Republic of Korea) were allies of the North America Alliance on paper but with the historic Titan terraforming contract going to a North American-based multinational, that relationship would be tested. Command had no idea why the Uju Kauboi was lurking around in deep space but they had watched their every move— which was how Halley knew exactly how to find them.

The large silver-white cosmoship cruiser was half the size of the Tyson and looked more aerodynamic, though that was irrelevant in space. The vessel had a standard ship design with a center larger rectangular passenger section and three gravity rings encircling the long main body; a tethered forward navigation and operations section; and a tethered Helios engine section at the rear. As he approached their vessel, he realized that their bridge might be wondering why an American military shuttle was cruising toward them.

"KCS Uju Kauboi Command, this is the NCS Gharial. Requesting permission for docking. No existing entry codes but need to speak with you regarding an urgent matter."

"NCS Gharial. You are from the NCS Neil deGrasse Tyson?"

"KCS Command, that is an affirmative."

"NCS Gharial, what is your urgent matter?"

"KCS Command, I'd prefer not to discuss on the open comm. I'll explain immediately upon boarding."

"NCS Gharial, stand by."

Halley didn't like it. His weapons were cold. His propulsion was off. He was literally a metal target hanging in space for any of their rail guns to blow to bits. The image was locked in his mind, and not because he had just done the same thing to an unknown hostile. It was the fear of any pilot in the service. Never be a sitting target in space without the ability to move or defend yourself. He was now breaking both those pilot commandments.

"NCS Gharial, what is your crew complement?" It was a different voice.

"KCS Command, only one. Myself. USS Army. Just bring me aboard Command. I will explain completely."

"NCS Gharial, stand by."

Halley was annoyed now, but all he could do was wait. The wait seemed to last forever.

"NCS Gharial, permission for docking granted." A third female voice.

Halley was now very worried. A pilot would never

hear more than one voice from docking command. Because of the unusual circumstances, he could rationalize a second. But three different bridge crew members taking turns to speaking to one shuttle? What the hell was going on over there?

"KCS Command, received and understood. Beginning docking approach now."

Halley sat in his chair as the Command computer took control for final docking. His vessel turned to its port side as it floated forward for the final docking. His trained ears heard the click, seal, and pressurizing. The steady green light shone on the cockpit display and around the shuttle's two doorways. He left the cockpit but was uneasy about stepping outside the ship.

The door opened and two members of the Kauboi's receiving crew waited: a male and female in black uniforms and armed with electro-rifles. The artificial grav line was right outside these new cruisers, so he walked out freely.

Halley made eye contact with them as soon the door opened. He knew something was very wrong. Their faces were covered with sweat, and their eyes—were wild. If these two came onto his ship and he was on Receiving, he wouldn't clear them for boarding.

"You are aboard the KCS Uju Kauboi." It was the second voice he'd heard on the comm.

Both of them noticed his expression.

Halley looked at the woman. "My memory with ranks in the Korean armed forces is not so good. What is your rank, ma'am?"

She stared at him. She knew what he was doing.

"Ma'am?" Halley repeated. "I am a lieutenant in the USS Army. You?"

"I am cadet. I have no rank."

He was certain that hers was the same female voice he'd heard on the comm. Why was the bridge crew greeting arrivals? Halley could feel his stomach sink. He pushed past them. "Where is your Command?"

It was a different class of ship and from another country but the basic design was always the same. He ran to the lift. Incredibly, he entered and the door closed without one of the other soldiers entering. He didn't have to read the Korean symbols on the side. A monkey could have guessed the right button to push for the command deck, and that was no insult to monkeys. The lift moved much faster than those on the Tyson.

Halley exited the lift, expecting to run into security. He saw no one. Now he was panicking. A glass door automatically slid open and closed behind him as he walked up metal stairs. The color pattern was a muted silver.

Up another set of metal stairs, the doors opened as he ran into the Control Room. He stopped.

The commanding officer sat in the conn with his back to him. To his left were about two dozen people in red jumpsuits. None of the bridge stations were manned. Halley looked around the room, then at the faces of the people. They were the same sweaty faces and scared eyes as what he'd witnessed upon arriving. Some were visibly shaking.

The doors opened again.

"Intruder!" a man yelled as he ran in, pointing his rifle at Halley. It was the same man who had greeted him at the docking bay.

Halley angrily grabbed the rifle from him as the same woman entered the Control Room. She stopped and stood in shock, as if expecting Halley to shoot them.

"Don't you ever, ever point a weapon at a senior

officer!" Halley yelled.

Halley threw the rifle into the KCS man's chest. The man caught it in his arms instinctively and trained his gaze on the ground. "Yes, sir. Sorry, sir."

Halley felt overwhelmed. He collected himself and walked to the front of the conn.

The commanding officer sat in the chair, staring out the main observation bay window as if in a trance. Halley stood to attention and saluted.

"Lieutenant Joshua Halley, USS Army reporting, sir. Permission to come aboard your ship."

The gesture snapped the man out of his trance. Halley didn't recognize his rank but he had to be a very senior officer of some kind. The man slowly saluted back.

"Permission granted." The commanding officer looked shell-shocked.

Halley glanced around again. "Sir, where is everyone? Where is your crew?"

He realized that the ship was actually on Red Alert but the lights were configured differently and there were no audible sounds.

The hell with it! They can shoot me if they want!

Halley ran to Tactical, then Sensors. He looked at the Watch station. He stepped to the display. Everyone who lived and worked in space had transponders for ship sensors to track. Halley felt sick and had to grab the sides of the console to steady himself. The sensors were tracking transponders floating in open space away from the Kauboi.

"Oh my God!" Halley yelled.

◆ ◆ ◆

"Where's the Medical Officer?" Halley asked, yelling at the junior officers.

"She's gone too," the man said.

"Come here!" Halley grabbed the man and pushed the woman out the front door. He turned back and looked at the people in jumpsuits. "I need you to pull yourselves together and as many of you as possible to follow me! We're going to try to save as many as we can!"

"We can't," one of the people in red said. "They're gone."

"They're not gone yet. They have these, don't they?"

Halley pointed to the zero-belt on his waist.

Everyone looked at their own zero-belts around their waists. Different ship, different country, same standard mandatory gear.

"One of you will be the pilot and I'll get them. I have my super-suit with me. You fly to them and I can pull them inside. But we have to hurry!"

The likelihood that Halley could recover all two hundred bodies was good. All personnel had their subcutaneous transponders so sensors would lead them to all of them. However, how many of them would still be alive? Invariably, some were already dead, but Halley didn't care.

"If we can find one person alive, it will be worth it!" Halley yelled, leading the officers to the launch bay. Thankfully, he didn't need them to take him there. He was taking them there.

They all piled out of the lift—Halley along with two black-uniformed officers and three of the red-uniformed people.

"How many pilots do I have?"

"I am one," the uniformed man said. "She can pilot too."

"I can pilot," said one of the men in red.

"I wish more of the others came with us, but we'll make do. I'll get into my super-suit and go with you." Halley pointed to the male officer. "The rest of you board and launch now. Stop the trajectory of those farthest away first. I'm the only one who will be outside, so help me. The easier you make it for me, the quicker I can get a person into the shuttle. You'll have to use your med-kit on them right away. We won't stop until we get everyone."

"Hi!"

Halley knew the grunt of acknowledgment was unique to the Asian countries. Every country had theirs. As long as they acknowledged him. For now, their fear and panic were gone. They had a purpose. Who knew how long it would take, but none of them would stop until the task was done.

◆ ◆ ◆

Halley's super-suit made him look like a robot killing

machine, adding at least five inches to his height—shiny, blue faceplate, built-in jet-pack, integrated rifles and bayonets. He boarded the shuttle and they launched. He didn't understand Korean, but he knew exactly what they were saying. Military protocols were the same. He recognized the voice of their commanding officer directing them.

There was nothing more terrorizing to any space explorer than the concept of being spaced. It was the nightmare in the back of everyone's mind, which was why everyone wore their zero-belt at all times—bed, shower, head, everywhere. If the unthinkable ever did happen, the zero-belt was one's only lifeline. It was rumored that some countries put cyanide needles in theirs, but Halley never believed that. A zero-belt function was simple: provide air for fifteen to thirty minutes so one could get rescued. After that, it wouldn't matter because you'd be dead.

Space was a peaceful place. Beautiful and hypnotic. But it could also be so scary, unforgiving, and deadly. Halley could see the next most terrorizing thing in a space explorer's life. The sight of someone who'd been spaced—in this case, dozens and dozens of bodies were fast approaching in their view. He took a deep breathe to psych himself out and prepare for the horrors he was about to see. Halley closed the cockpit door, sealing it from the rear compartment. He then opened the bay door and both the screeching warning and flashing lights began. He hoped the pilot knew how to bypass. He did; both stopped. The door opened to space. Halley rocketed out of the shuttle's rear compartment.

He had made a mental note of the KCS shuttle with the extra man. That was the one where a survivor had their best chance. Two personnel to try to revive and save people rather than one.

Halley grabbed his first and second bodies at almost the same time. He was going to have nightmares about it for a while. They were like frozen zombies in space— their skin and uniforms glistened with a coat of thin ice. At least their eyes were closed and it was clear that they had time to use the devices on their zero-belts. He had to think of them as not human but as cargo he had to grab and dash into the shuttles. If he thought of them as human beings, he would not be able to do the job.

He filled one shuttle with floating bodies, closed its bay door, and quickly flew around to signal the pilot through the cockpit window. He moved to fill the next shuttle, moving quicker, and establishing a rhythm to the grim work. He had to push all stray thoughts of him working in an endless ocean of black and ignore the lights of the Kauboi in the distance. He pushed more bodies into the second shuttle.

He would try to cram many, many more in the last shuttle because that would be the one he'd get into as well to help the female officer. The two of them would be the absolute last hope for any who could be revived. He already accepted that any other bodies that he couldn't get into the last shuttle, he'd leave. After they attempted to revive survivors, they could recover the remaining corpses later.

When he got into the third shuttle, he flew inside and closed it. Halley estimated that there were about another hundred or more souls floating away. The cockpit opened up and the female officer rushed out with the med-kits. They would have to move quickly to try to revive body after body in zero-gravity. It was the best they could do; it was all they could do.

◆ ◆ ◆

Halley sat in the cockpit with the female soldier as she raced back to the Kauboi. He could feel his resolve cracking as tears welled up in his eyes. All he thought about was the hundred or so other soldiers floating helplessly in the void of space.

"They come! Cavalry!" the female soldier yelled, pointing.

While they were gone, those aboard had been working, too. All base cruisers had bots for external maintenance. Several of them raced by, toward the other bodies with their three slender robotic arms extended.

Halley began to stand so that he could put on his helmet. "I could help."

Something was holding down his left arm. It was the female soldier. "You have done your duty, sir. It's their turn," she said.

As Halley sat back down, he saw the fourth shuttle they'd left behind pass them, already with its cargo bay open to space. They didn't have super-suits like his but UROK had their own space suits that could handle the task.

When they stepped across the gravity line after docking, not only did they feel their weight again, but the fatigue and exhaustion hit them all at once. Other red uniforms ran to their shuttle for the bodies of their comrades. They had more advanced med-kits, floating bio-beds, and a multi-armed floating battlefield med-bot that he was certain they had activated for the first time. The Tyson had one too, somewhere. No one in the military used battle med-bots anymore. He even saw one of the red uniforms reviewing the instructions on his tablet.

"I just need to close my eyes for a bit," he said.

He suddenly felt the female soldier helping him walk to the lift. There, a red uniform helped, too. The tech said something in Korean and the lift began moving. It was a preference of command as to whether a ship was touch-button or voice-command. He and Capt. Ayla preferred touch-button. Use those muscles, lazy human.

They took him to the captain's mess.

"Thanks, I'm fine now." Halley walked into the private dining room, found a corner, and laid down. He was out like a light, still clutching his helmet in one hand. Super-suits were very comfortable for sleeping, too.

Halley had no idea how long he had been sleeping. When he got up, he stumbled to the sink in the mess, opened the tap, cupped a glove, and splashed water on his face.

With his knowledge of military vessels, he knew exactly where to go to find the sick bay. But he stopped. The sick bay would be too small for two hundred bodies. He found the lift to the general mess. If such a catastrophe happened on the Tyson, the first thing they would do was transform the general mess into a larger sick bay.

Halley marched in and found that the situation was as he had guessed. The two black-uniformed soldiers were on guard as red uniforms were busy at work. The battle med-bot was flying all around under close supervision. All the dead bodies were lined up on their backs, row after row, covered with a blankets or large towels. Halley felt the pain in his gut as if it were his own crew. They were soldiers and didn't deserve to die the way they had.

He noticed partitions in the corner and perked up. He looked at the two soldiers. "Survivors?" he asked.

The male soldier smiled. "You saved them, sir," he replied.

"We saved them. How many?"

"Twenty fully recovered and twenty-two will recover."

Not even half but forty-two was forty-two saved.

"Lieutenant, Senior Officer Yobi wishes to see you. He waits in Control."

Halley nodded. Looking at himself, he realized he was still in his super-suit, but he had no desire to get out of it.

He had come to the Uju Kauboi for a reason. He had no idea how much time had passed. He had abandoned his crew on the Tyson only to be thrust into saving the crew of another ship. The doors auto-opened as he walked into the Control Room. The commanding officer stood from the conn to face him. The man was the only one in the room. He smiled at Halley, almost a laugh.

"You saved my crew, sir. I am unworthy of this ship and this military. I lost the crew and if I had done what you did, I could have saved them. Your quick action saved forty-two members of my crew. My lack of action killed one hundred forty-two members of my crew—not the invaders. I am a disgrace to this uniform, the Kauboi, and my country. I relinquish command to you, Lieutenant Joshua Halley."

"Sir, it was a horrific accident."

The male and female Korean officers entered the Control Room as Halley watched the senior officer suck on the barrel of a pistol and blow his brains out of his skull.

Chapter Five

Relieved of Duty

None of them had ever seen a ship blown up in space before, not even the Sarge, and he'd been in the Army forever. Most Marines had never seen it and they blew up things for a living, along with shooting big guns.

Medical Officer Lieutenant Carina McAuliffe hadn't been aboard the Tyson a long time. For the Titan mission, the Company wanted someone with a multitude of advanced degrees, as well as ambitious and young. Six months later and most of the crew, Army and Navy, still knew relatively little about her. Some thought of her as a plant for the Company, but actually she was supposed to be the ears and eyes of Planet Tamers. That was her job. The health and mental well-being of the crew.

She had arrived in the Control Room and began

looking over the bridge crew. Captain Ayla sat quietly in her chair, already knowing what was coming.

"Skipper, I'm going to have to temporarily relieve your Sensors and Tactical officers of duty."

Captain Ayla didn't look at the doctor. She stared off in the distance.

"Watch, please have the next ensigns on duty report immediately," Commander Cassiopeia said to the ensign at the station.

In less than a minute, two new ensigns entered the room. The Command pointed the replacements to their station. She looked at the relieved junior officers standing together. "Ensigns, you are relieved. Please go to your quarters."

On the verge of tears, the ensign on Sensors couldn't wait to get out of the Control Room. The ensign on Tactical stormed out of the room, mad.

Lieutenant Centaurus and the Sarge stood quietly nearby. Relieving personnel of duty was one of the jobs a commanding officer tried to avoid at all costs.

"Captain, may I speak with you privately?" Lieutenant McAuliffe asked.

Ayla shot an evil look at her. She slowly stood. "The captain's mess."

"I'll follow," the doctor said.

"Commander, you have the conn," Captain Ayla said.

"Yes, ma'am."

"Do you want us here or wait below?" Lieutenant Centaurus asked her.

"Here is fine," Ayla said. "Maybe you can help my ensigns determine why our sensors couldn't locate that hostile but Lieutenant Halley could."

"He likely had line-of-sight on the vessel, ma'am," Sarge said to her.

"Yeah. Commander, does anyone on our crew have combat experience of any kind?"

"No, ma'am."

"No? That's it. You've reviewed every file of our two hundred personnel already?"

"Ma'am, you know we don't."

She looked at Army. "Lieutenant, anyone in your crew?"

"No, ma'am."

"That's not entirely true," Sarge interjected.

"Who?" Lieutenant Centaurus asked.

"Halley," the Sarge answered.

"I know the C.O.'s file. There's nothing in there about combat."

"It's why he got this gig."

"What are you talking about?" Ayla asked.

"How do you know this? It's not in his file," Lieutenant Centaurus said.

"I heard...people talking," Sarge said. "That's how I know, and I don't know why it's not in his file."

"Halley has combat experience?" Captain Ayla asked.

"Yes."

"So, the only person on the Tyson who knows how to kill people and blow shit up is now no longer on the Tyson when we absolutely need him to be, and we'll probably never see again."

"Don't say that," Centaurus said. "He'll be back. Remember, he probably saved our butts."

"I know that, Lieutenant. Yes, I'm sorry. I'm sure it's another black mark against me with the doc. While I'm gone, do we think we can get a plan together?"

"Will do, ma'am," Commander Cassiopeia replied.

"The Sarge and I will focus on defense. If there was one ship, there might be more."

"We're due to touch down on Titan in six months," Captain Ayla said to herself. "Orders. Arrived?"

"No, ma'am," the commander answered.

"Are we being jammed?" Ayla asked.

"We'll figure it out, ma'am."

"Captain."

"Yes, yes. Follow me, Doctor."

Captain Ayla led their medical officer out of the Control Room.

Lieutenant Centaurus and the Sarge looked at each other. Commander Cassiopeia noticed them and wasn't happy either.

♦ ♦ ♦

"You have no authority," Ayla said coldly.

The women sat in the captain's small but private dining room. The doctor expected the response and remained calm.

"I will not relieve you temporarily of duty but I will insist that you rest for at least four hours—"

"Two!"

"Rest for two hours without interruption. Your X.O. and the Army can handle things for two hours."

"Doctor, you do realize that I'm the most senior person aboard."

"On the Navy side. Army Staff Sergeant Ogun is the other. I'll speak to the Lieutenant and make sure he's on hand on the bridge."

"This is unacceptable."

"You're right. I'm only a medical officer. I've been here six months. I have no idea about military command structure in practical terms, not what they teach in a classroom far from reality. But what I do know is that people who are under severe stress that they cannot handle can freeze at the very moment when life-saving decisions need to be made. I know how dangerous this situation is. That's why I'm doing this. I'm hoping—I'm praying—that Lieutenant Halley's act buys us the time we need to pull everyone together. Six months is a long time, Captain. Can you command your ship in that time?"

"If not me, who?"

"Fair question, which is why I'm agreeing to two hours. It's in my authority to relieve you of your duties until the completion of a full psych eval, but notice I didn't mention that. Mandatory rest is all. I'll even do the same for the two ensigns I relieved. Though, they'll probably never want to return to the bridge."

"I agree with that."

"But I'll be on the bridge too from now on. You can roll your eyes all you want but do you think it's appropriate for Navy officers to burst out crying on the bridge?"

"They're kids."

"They're junior officers. This is the scientists' bargain, Captain. If you want to be a scientist in space, you have to join the military. You can be a scientist most of the time but when the time comes, you must be military."

"What about you, Doctor? Have you come close to combat?"

"I'm hurt that you don't remember my file."

"I delegate review of crew files to my X.O."

"Not sure how wise that is, ma'am, but to answer your question, no. Grew up in a very dangerous neighborhood but that doesn't count."

"Why are you on the Tyson then?"

"Like you, Captain, it's about the mission. Titan is why I'm here. We terraform Titan and I'll probably never leave. That's why I need you to get your head on straight, get your crew together. I never saw a ship destroyed in space either."

"None of us have."

"I'd rather never see it again. I'd rather it not be us next time. You do your job, captain, and I'll help you do it, any way I can. I'm not here to babysit you but and I'm not here to undermine you, either. I report to you."

"What do you think I should do then? After my two-hour house arrest."

The lieutenant smirked. "Time for the Navy and Army to be Navy-Army."

"That's what Halley would do."

"He'll be back. He will."

"He'd better. I've waited over a decade to find an Army C.O. I could work with and not want to gag when I saw them coming. I'm not going to let him get away so easily with this mission of a lifetime."

Chapter Six

Incoming Call

The Tyson remained on General Quarters. Centaurus and Sarge double-timed through the Army section, yelling out orders.

"Look at what I'm seeing," Sarge said to the Lieutenant.

Corporal Yuri led Privates Zapata and Balkan with a dozen enlisted behind them. Every man was armed with an electro-rifle, except Balkan, who carried the menacing "quad-shooter"—one gun, four barrels, eight shots with one trigger pull.

"Lieutenant," Corporal Yuri began, "we're ready for it."

"Yes, Corporal, I see that, which is what worries me."

"Minotaur, why are you carrying the quad-shooter?"

Sarge yelled. "Do you know something the L.T. and I don't know?"

"We're under attack, Sarge," Corporal Yuri said. "Everyone on board is talking about it. How many times did the enemy vessel fire on us before the C.O. blasted them out of space?"

"Hurrah!" the men yelled in unison.

"Navy said they tried to sneak aboard and space their sailors," Private Zapata said.

"Where are you getting this info, soldier? No one was spaced. And no enemy vessel fired on the Tyson," Lieutenant Centaurus corrected.

"But the C.O. did blow them up, right, sir?" Yuri asked.

"Yes, that part is true," the LT answered.

"Hurrah!" the men yelled in unison.

"How many intruders do we think are aboard, sir?" another private asked.

"There are no intruders aboard!" the LT yelled. "Not even aliens."

The men got deadly quiet.

"I'm not being serious," the LT quickly said.

"Aliens, sir?" the private asked.

"Private, listen good. There are no intruders, and no aliens. Nothing."

The men looked at the Lieutenant. As if they didn't believe him.

"Soldiers, you know the routine. Get to your posts ASAP!" the Sarge yelled. "You don't know 'em, shoot 'em. Go, go, go!"

The men raced back down the corridor. The one private glanced back at them, then disappeared around the corner.

"Sir, I really wish you didn't say that," the Sarge said.

"Why?"

"I know your sense of humor. They don't. Did you see their faces? When they're in that state, no jokes, no booze, no coffee, no stimulants, and no wild ideas of any kind. We need them rational. Young soldiers have overactive imaginations already. No need to amplify them anymore. That one crack will fuel rumors for days. We better pray nothing else happens."

"What else could happen?"

"You're kidding me, right, sir?"

"You don't really believe in aliens?"

"I neither believe nor disbelieve. What I do know is that you don't know either. We're out here in deep space. Humans haven't been out here before."

"If there were aliens, don't you think we'd know by now? Gotten a 'how 'bout a fist bump hello' already?"

"Why? Terran monkeys mucking around on their own home planet. Why would I visit that? Nothing impressive about that."

"We've been on the moon."

"So? The Terran monkeys can hop from their home planet to the orbiting moon. Maybe the aliens got marsupials on their planet that can do the same."

"Sarge, that's crazy. We're on Mars."

"I say Terran monkeys start to get interesting when they start flying to other planets and terraforming them into habitable planets. If I were them, that's when I'd start to take notice and maybe want to drop a crop circle on someone or find some cows."

"There's nothing out here, Sarge, but us."

"And the hostile that Bogeyman blasted out of space. Forgot already?"

"We were heading to the Engine Section."

"Yes, we were, sir. I'd say we get there as fast as we can. The C.O. isn't out there to blow up any more stealth ships for us."

◆ ◆ ◆

At full-burn, the trip from Earth to Saturn and Titan was two years with the most advanced piece of mover technology ever made—the Helios engine. Anything engineering asked for they got—from the skipper, Command, and the Company. However, this time the request would be the other way.

The man in charge was Gremlin. Tech Sergeant Shaw Klang had held the post for five years. He had served in engine rooms on Terran subs and aerial cruisers, cosmoships in all three branches of the space services, and even in other governments besides those in the North American Alliance. He might have known everything there was to know about the Tyson, but he knew everything and more about the Helios engine.

Some speculated that he even had the classified knowledge to build one himself if he had to, which was why the Company had put him on the Tyson. He looked young but he was older than everyone on the ship, except maybe the Sarge.

The LT and Sarge stepped off the elevator at the rearmost connecting neck to the Engine section. The junction was always heavily guarded but with General Quarters had double the security.

"L.T., Sarge," they greeted.

"Sailors," the LT said.

The lieutenant and sergeant found Tech Sergeant Klang in his office reviewing energy reports. He looked up from his desk as they entered the spacious room with monitors and screens everywhere.

"Tech Sarge, we don't get down to the underworld often enough," Sarge said.

"That's Army talk, Sarge. My domain is known as the ship's ass."

The Sarge laughed.

"Tech sarge, do you know what's been happening?" the LT asked.

"I know everything."

"Then we came to the right place. The Sarge and I need to know how to detect a ship that vanished from our sensors. If there was one, we fear there may be others," Lieutenant Centaurus said. "Navy is upgrading the sensors but they're star scientists, planet scientists. Upgrade a sensor to see a star or black hole, that's them. To see a ship hiding and hunting you, not so confident."

"L.T., the only way to see a ship with that kind of stealth tech is line of sight. Augment the sensors with cameras. Position them to cover every vantage point and blind spot on the ship, so no place to hide. Sometimes low tech is the best defense against high tech."

"Cameras?" the LT asked.

"It'll take a helluva long time but attach cameras over the Tyson's entire hull," Klang said.

"We'll get started right away then," the Lieutenant said.

"I'll have my crew help but start with the engine section first."

The LT and Sarge grinned. "Of course," Sarge said.

"Then it would make sense to do the command

section next," Klang said.

"Thanks for the permission, Tech Sergeant," the LT said.

"I do have one question, though, and no offense, L.T., since you're now Army C.O., but where did Halley go?" Klang asked.

♦ ♦ ♦

"Downgrade to Yellow Alert Readiness status," Captain Ayla said.

"Yes, captain," Commander Cassiopeia responded.

Captain Ayla stood at her station next to the Control Room's conn. The commander typed in the new directive and the flashing Red Alert became a steady yellow light on the wall. "Attention, crew. This is the captain. Maintain Yellow Readiness status and man your stations until further notice," she said into a mic for the overhead.

A new junior lieutenant was on Tactical. The brother and sister team of Ensigns Rosen-bridge and Kirkwood were on Sensors (or "Eyes") and the Watch station, respectively. Lieutenant McAuliffe—the doctor—stood at the corner of the Watch station, trying to be as inconspicuous as possible. Behind the conn, the Sarge stood quietly, a rifle in hand.

"Captain, do you really want me here on the bridge?" he asked.

"Oh, don't feel unwanted, Sarge," Captain Ayla said. "This is one time Navy is happy to have Army on the bridge. When sensors are upgraded as much as possible and with your little cameras mounted on the hull, then we'll all be able to breathe a bit easier."

Lieutenant Centaurus entered the Control Room. He looked at the Sarge. "The bots are almost done with the engine section, then they'll be here. I'd say another hour."

"How many crews at work?" the Sarge asked.

"All hands on deck, Sarge. No one sleeps until the work is done," the LT answered.

"Good."

Commander Cassiopeia touched her earpiece. The bridge could hear the incoming audio indicator. "Captain, we have an incoming encrypted message from the...KCS Uju Kauboi."

"The Koreans," Sarge said.

"The Space Cowboy," the LT added. He saw the doctor's face. "That's Korean."

"Yes, Lieutenant, I know. It's one of the six languages I speak."

"Six languages?" The Lieutenant was impressed. "I speak only three."

"Where are they?" the captain asked.

"Our side of Jupiter but not moving."

"Who's commanding their ship?"

Commander Cassiopeia typed something on her station's keyboard. "KCS Uju Kauboi, Argonaut-class base cruiser, commanded by a UROK Colonel Hikaru Yobi, ma'am."

"Captain, Argonaut-class? I thought we were the only ones out here in deep space," Dr. McAuliffe said to the captain.

"No, lieutenant, they're out here too but we're the only ones on the way to Titan. No one owns space, lieutenant—at least not yet."

"Why are they here?" the doctor asked.

"Let me take their call and I'll ask them." Captain

Ayla touched a button on her panel to activate the tiny view screen and her mouth opened in surprise. "Halley!"

The entire bridge looked at her. The LT and Sarge ran to her station, followed by everyone else.

"Lieutenant Halley, you are not UROK Colonel Hikaru Yobi. We didn't expect to see you for some time. You did promise that we'd see you on Titan."

"Captain, please excuse your non-command crew members. LT?"

"Yes, sir," Lieutenant Centaurus replied.

"Who's there for us?"

"Just the Sarge."

"That's fine, Captain?"

The captain looked at the ensigns who both looked at Ayla, vigorously shaking their heads. "Sorry, ensigns. Wait outside in the hallway. Dismissed but only temporarily."

The two ensigns grudgingly left.

"Lieutenant McAuliffe."

"Dr. McAuliffe is staying put."

"Lieutenant Halley, the doctor won't leave. Should I have her forcibly removed?"

"That won't be necessary. Is the bridge free?"

"Free and clear, except for us five."

"Let me mention from the outset that what I'm about to say shouldn't be shared with the general crew."

"Why?" both Captain Ayla and Lieutenant Centaurus asked at the same time.

"Where's their C.O.?" Captain Ayla asked. "I can guess why you're aboard but not why you're on their bridge comm."

"Senior Officer Yobi is dead."

The words hit the Tyson command crew with a wave of shock.

"Suicide."

"What?" Ayla called out. Such a thing was impossible for a command officer. The doctor's mouth hung open. The news shocked her more than the others.

"I came aboard…well you know why. If I'm going to the Belt Colonies, maybe I could hitch a ride. Also, have them do a sensor sweep for any more hostiles.

"I'm sorry to say that this story will get far worse before it gets better. It seems their ship was also visited by a Dolphin-class-like shuttle with all the right entry codes. Only they let them aboard. About one hour later, the KCS Uju Kaubi suffered a catastrophic event."

"What kind of event, Halley?" Ayla asked.

"All crew not on the bridge at the time were...ejected into space."

"Oh my God," the commander said.

For a while, no one spoke.

"Do you need assistance, Josh?" Lieutenant Centaurus asked. "There'd be no shortage of volunteers to get to you right now."

"Negative, Lieutenant. As horrific as this is, it has nothing to do with the Tyson or our mission. I found myself leading the rescue effort. We managed to save forty-two of their crew."

"Good work, sir," the Sarge said.

"But that still leaves more than half deceased, though we recovered all the bodies. The reason I'm calling is not to give you this night's share of nightmares."

"I doubt any of us will be sleeping for a while after this," Captain Ayla said.

"This week's nightmares, sir," Sarge added.

"The shuttle I destroyed was not the shuttle that did this to the Kauboi," Halley said.

"It's still out there?" Lieutenant Centaurus said.

"It is. The choices are: It's following us, meaning the Kauboi, or it's following you, or it's going to wherever its base ship is. That means another large cruiser is out here. It's my duty to make sure you know."

"Halley, what do you plan to do?" Captain Ayla asked.

"I have my own mission, Captain, and I'm going to complete it no matter what. You have yours."

"Halley, you got to get back here," Ayla said.

"What about their ship?" the Sarge asked.

"There are two junior officers here with me. A grand total of one year of active military service between them, but I'm going to get them squared away. And I'm going to make sure the ship is safe. You make sure the Tyson is safe."

"We're less than six months from Titan and I've been in space for fifteen years and I've never seen or heard of anything like this. All on one day. What's going to happen tomorrow? I have a radical thought, Halley."

"I know, Captain. I had the same one fifteen minutes ago but there's no way. This ship has to get to a space base, immediately. That's the only trip this Kauboi will be making. Tyson, signing out."

"Sir, wait!" Lieutenant Centaurus yelled.

Halley was gone from the screen.

"Now, we're definitely not seeing him until we get to Titan," Captain Ayla said.

Chapter Seven

Kauboi Halley

The clean-up was painful to watch. Young red uniforms—kids just out of training school—cleaning blood and brain matter from the floor and stations of the Kauboi's Control Room. Several of them worked quietly but thoroughly.

The man Yobi had committed suicide right in front of him. Halley wondered if such a thing could have happened on any Earth Alliance ship—suicide. Neither soldier nor scientist would even know how to go about such a thing. It was so beyond their experiences or imagination. If you assigned it to them as a "task," they'd look at you perplexed for a while, thinking on all cylinders. They'd have to consult with others and they still wouldn't know how to go about it. Probably, they'd settle on the hackneyed "shoot yourself with a gun" approach only because they'd seen it in some movie. In real life, suicides in space never happened. Murders didn't happen in space. Violence didn't happen because deep space was managed by only soldiers and scientists. On Earth? The complete opposite. Civilians had the planet and there was plenty of all of it there.

Despite the stereotypes, even among space mining workers, violence against another or yourself was unheard of. Everyone living and working in deep space had every psych test and eval known to man. If you weren't cleared, you weren't going into space—period.

He was glad his soldiers "wouldn't know what to do." But Yobi knew what to do. The man moved smoothly and without fear, as if he'd done it a million times. Halley didn't know much of Korean culture and hoped that suicide wasn't a common thing in their Mil-Sci. But he did know that some cultures on Earth valued personal and family honor above everything else. In Halley's mind, even a disgraced life would be a life worth living. However, maybe to Senior Officer Yobi such a life would be worse than death. Maybe in his world the shame to the family or the uniform was worthy of a death sentence.

Halley shook his head to stop dwelling on the horrific deed. Instead, his mind drifted to another problem. Navy was more superstitious than Army but most space explorers were. For instance, no ship was ever launched on a day when a spaceship had been destroyed or a space explorer had been killed in space en route. Centuries later and no ship was ever launched on 27th January—marking America's first catastrophic event with the deaths of the first three astronauts of Apollo 1, or 28th January, when the Space Shuttle Challenger exploded killing all seven of its crew aboard, including a civilian teacher. In fact, the maiden launch of any cosmoship never occurred on a day a space explorer—of any country—died in space or getting there.

What happened today to the Uji Kauboi would haunt the Koreans forever too. But as an officer, he did not envy the Kauboi's next commanding officer. If they were anything like American crews, the ship's crew could grow to think the ship was cursed. Once a crew got such a thing in their minds, the good running of any ship and its morale was finished. He would never know the crushing despair and shame Yobi felt that caused the soldier to end his own life the way he did, but he inadvertently made life untenable for those on the Kauboi. Who would want to serve aboard a ship whose crew had been spaced and whose commanding blew his brains out at the conn?

The man likely had a spotless record. One didn't

become the commanding officer of a nation's flagship by being anything less. All his accomplishments and honors would be erased by a horrific incident that no soldier could anticipate. But the commanding officer must anticipate everything. You got the accolades for the wins but also the blame for the disasters. That was the order of things just as much today as it had been in the past and would be in the future.

"What is burial protocol for senior officers in your military services?" Halley asked, seated in the conn.

The two junior officers stood at his side.

"He will be buried on Earth, sir," the male one replied. Lieutenant Hajime was his name.

"With honors?" Halley asked.

The lieutenants remained quiet.

Halley sighed loudly. He didn't imagine Korean Command would behave any differently from his own. Commanding Officer Yobi would be lucky if his body ever reached Earth after such a disaster, and that was what it would be called. To lose over a hundred soldiers in one day. All of UROK would be mourning for years or longer. Unthinkable.

He looked at the junior officers. "Lieutenant Hajime

and Lieutenant Yi-so-yeon, I don't have the authority—
"

"You do, sir," Lieutenant Hajime corrected. "You are senior officer of the Uji Kauboi."

"Then you both are senior officers as far as I am concerned." He looked at the red uniforms, some on all fours on the floor. "Okay, enough of that. The Command Room is clean enough, dismissed."

The red uniforms moved quickly out of the bridge.

"Lieutenants, there are only three of us so between us we have five stations to man. First thing, Lieutenant Hajime, I want you to raise your Command on comms. Immediately."

"Yes, sir." The junior office ran to the station.

"Second, I want every sensor looking for the hostile that did this. Immediately."

"Yes, sir." Lieutenant Yi-so-yeon ran to the Sensors station.

"We find that hostile, then I'll defer to you both to make the kill."

The two junior officers looked at each other. They didn't know whether to smile.

"Hi! Yes, sir!" they said in unison and returned to carry out their orders.

◆ ◆ ◆

For Earth-based military services, basic training was three months long and Advanced Individual Training (AIT) was an additional year. But the action for most was space—Military Science. Its services made up over seventy percent of the armed forces. Advanced training for space lasted at least three years. Grunts in the modern Army were better trained than ever in the history of Earth—both a blessing and a curse. A brand new officer or enlisted rotated to their first duty station with four to five years of training under their belt. However, as Halley saw in the faces of his two new command junior officers, classroom training, no matter how good, could not and would never replace real in-the-field experience.

No experience, however, could prepare even the seasoned officer for the horror of a ship's crew spaced. Even before Halley had joined up, he had seen his fair share of "pandorum syndrome" reels, wherein some crazy spaceman spaces his own crew. Only once in AIT had they been told there was no such thing. However, "space dementia" was very real, albeit rare, and could make the urban myth a reality.

Halley wondered if they had the same reels in Korea and if his new command junior officers had seen them, too. For the moment, they had new duties and horror shows, real or fantasy, had to be pushed aside in their minds. The emotion hit Halley all at once as he sat in the conn. Nothing would stop him from getting to the Belt Colonies and then Uroboros, but he had to accept the fact that, for his father, it was already too late.

Lieutenant Hajime had finally reached UROK Command. Halley heard hushed words in Korean and then the young ensign nervously looked up at him.

"Do you need me to leave the room, lieutenants?" Halley asked.

The junior officer said nothing as they looked at each other as if to gather their courage.

"I'll stand in the hall."

Halley did so. Outside the Control Room, he sat on the floor. At the end of the corridor were two red uniformed tech acting as military guards. The poor souls had probably handled a weapon once in basic training and then never again—assuming they had gone through military training at all. They might have been civilian techs only transferred to the military for service.

The door to the Control Room opened and Lieutenant Yi-so-yeon bowed her head as she gestured him back in. Lieutenant Hajime gestured for Halley to sit as he walked back to the Helm and pushed a button.

Halley sat and got comfortable as a white-haired man appeared on his desk screen. Lieutenant Yi-so-yeon appeared next to him and tapped the screen. It popped up and she angled it so that Halley would have the best view. Both junior officers walked to the farthest station to wait.

The man was an even more senior officer but not a general. "Who am I addressing?" he asked.

"Lieutenant Joshua Halley of the NCS Neil deGrasse Tyson, sir."

"Operation Fairy Dancer, is it?"

"Yes, sir. The Titan mission."

"The cadets briefed me on what happened."

"Yes, sir. I'm sorry for the tragedy."

"Yes, thank you."

"And that your command lost a command officer."

"I'm not. Had he returned, he would have been executed."

Halley kept his calm demeanor but the revelation shocked him.

"What are your intentions, Lieutenant Halley?"

"My intentions, sir?"

"The KCS Uju Kauboi is without its commanding officer, but you have ably taken charge of the situation and the ship."

"Sir, I'm a soldier and I was doing what I was trained to do. I'm sure you have another ship en route. Once they arrive and properly identify themselves to the lieutenants, I'll immediately relinquish the conn to them. I originally came aboard to get to the Belt Colonies."

"Are you not the Army commanding officer of the NCS Tyson?"

"I am, sir, but I have my own set of circumstances that required me to temporarily leave my ship."

"You mean Uroboros." Halley wasn't surprised that UROK Command knew about the incident. Most likely every government and region of Earth did by now.

"Yes, sir. Any intel you could provide would be appreciated."

"Of course. Unfortunately, our nearest military ship is months away. However, we have contracted with one of the mining ships nearby to shore up the Kauboi's crew."

"Very good, sir. With your permission, I'll alter course to rendezvous at maximum burn."

"Permission granted. Lieutenant Hajime has the new orders on the mining ship."

"Civilians, sir?"

"Yes."

"Do we anticipate any problems with their crew or command?"

The man smiled. "It is refreshing to speak with real military who knows what he's doing. We're going to pay them handsomely so there will no problems from them. But I would like you to assess them."

"Will do, sir."

"I cannot express to you the gratitude of my country

for your quick reaction to such a disaster. Many lives were saved, and your efforts will be duly recognized. I will personally call your space commander."

"Thank you, sir. Have the junior officers also told you of my concerns about the hostile and a possible base ship?"

"Yes, Lieutenant Yi-so-yeon did inform me and you already have her on those duties. There are no ships in your vicinity, but we have all our long-range sensors searching. If we detect any other ship, we will contact you immediately. The mining ship we are sending will be heavily armed."

"Very good, sir. And sir, what is your name?"

"I would be a Lieutenant Colonel in your services. Lieutenant Colonel Mecha."

"Thank you, sir."

"I can sleep well knowing that, despite this disaster, my country's flagship is in capable hands. I will have that intel sent to you. Good night, lieutenant—not that you'll be sleeping anytime soon."

"Yes, sir, and thank you."

Chapter Eight

Final Orders

Mil-Sci's "Operation Fairy Dancer." The largest endeavor ever for humankind since the nation-rebuilding plans and operations after Earth's World Wars. The terraforming of Titan was that big of a deal. It involved multiple countries, most of the Americas' armed services, and the entire space science community and was run by the largest multinational on Earth. Captain Ayla heard that the world's parliaments and legislative branches and the Company's board of directors got daily briefings.

Yes, they still hadn't gotten their final orders. They were T-minus six months from Saturn's largest moon, a planetary body about half the size of Earth but larger than our own Luna.

The Control Room had its own briefing room, but

Ayla never used it. Her predecessor had used it as his private sleeping room, and sleep he did most of the time. He was a lousy captain whom she was happy to see the back of. She was the ship's captain now.

"Co-captain," Centaurus said purposely, to annoy her.

"There is no such designation as co-captain, lieutenant. The Tyson is a science ship, not a military one. I am the captain of the ship. Halley, or you, sadly, are the captain of the military defense of the ship. I command the science stuff. You command the bang-bang-shoot-shoot stuff. I tried to dumb it down as much as I could. Didn't you learn this in AIT?"

"Captain, I wasn't being serious."

Ayala had assembled the same Tyson command staff: herself, Commander Cassiopeia, the LT, and the Sarge, but the doctor invited herself. "Yes, of course," she said. "I think we can all agree that we don't want to ever be caught off-guard again. It will be tough but we should remain on GQ status until Titan."

"I agree," Lieutenant Centaurus said. "I also think we should swap out your tactical and sensors with soldiers."

"Why?" Captain Ayla asked. "My sailors can push a button as easily as a soldier can."

"Captain, you have Symbiote and Sludge on those stations. Do I need to say more? They're scientists."

Ayala suppressed a look. "Who do you recommend?"

"Private Superjovian on Sensors—"

"Minotaur?" Captain Ayala and the Commander asked.

"He never talks," Captain Ayala said.

"An excellent trait for someone on Sensors, don't you think, captain?" the Sarge asked.

"Okay, and Tactical?"

"Private Sirius. Leo—"

"No! Absolutely not. He talks too much. I'll do double-duty and take Tactical. If Lieutenant Halley were here, he'd be all our choices. I'm sure you have Corporal Yuri leading the enlisted on our security."

"Yes," Lieutenant Centaurus answered.

"Then that's the crew assignments."

"Who will relieve you all for the other two watches?"

Lieutenant MacAuliffe asked.

"Commander, work on that. We'll staff shifts between us so that one of us is on at all times."

"Yes, ma'am."

"ETA on the camera retro-fit?" the captain asked.

"We should be done in two hours," Lieutenant Centaurus said.

"Gremlin also modified some of our bots to be in continuous flight alongside the ship," Sarge added.

"Excellent. Commander, that just leaves us with Sensors. Unfortunately, we won't know if the upgrades are worth a damn until something tries to sneak up on us and we see it."

"Do you think someone else will try to sneak up of us?" the doctor asked.

"Lieutenant, we're supposed to be the only ones out here between Jupiter and Saturn."

"What about our orders?" Lieutenant Centaurus asked. "Has the Admiral been in contact?"

"No. We're having issues with the signal," the captain answered.

The LT and Sarge exchanged looks.

"Shouldn't we be concerned about that?" the Sarge answered.

"I hear you, Sarge, but I'm not ready to jump on the paranoid train until we can definitely say that the signal is being jammed rather than there are technical difficulties on their end or the signal is being knocked out of space by cosmic rays. I've been on the Tyson for fifteen years. Not being able to get in touch with Command does happen. We actually pray for it. Granted, there's a sense of urgency."

"What do you think it all means, captain?" Sarge asked. "I'll just say it aloud because I know others are thinking it. Is the mission starting to go sideways?"

"Absolutely not. Nothing and no one is keeping us from our mission. We're on high alert. Everyone is armed. You have the camera retro-fit and upgraded sensors. Six months to go."

"There are rumors, captain. And what happened to the Uji Kauboi? Were they really going to do that to us?"

"Lieutenant Centaurus, please do not scare the command staff with that kind of speculation. The Tyson is in good hands. The Uji Kauboi is in good hands. We need to keep our wits about us. Let's keep the excess chatter to zero."

"With their overactive imaginations, we'd better," Lieutenant Centaurus said. "The Sarge and I will come up with drills to keep them busy."

"Yes, commander, see to that too for Navy. Lieutenant, that's all I have."

"Nothing more on my end, captain."

"Then let's get to Titan as quickly as we can without another incident."

◆ ◆ ◆

Ayala preferred to take the priority calls in the captain's mess. The face of Admiral Zed Antares appeared on screen at the corner of the desk.

"Admiral," Ayala greeted.

"Captain. Report."

"On GQ status, sir, and will be until Titan touchdown. Tyson suffered no damage from its encounter with the hostile. Army has retro-fitted the Tyson hull with physical cameras so we'll have twenty-four-hour line of sight. Also, we have modified bots in continuous flight alongside the ship."

"Have you determined what stealth tech the hostile had?"

"No, sir."

"Likely, they came from the Belt Colonies."

"Have others been attacked like this, sir?"

"Not like this, but there have been a few incidents. But it will be thoroughly investigated and handled, so I don't want you to concern yourself. Command also doesn't think there is any other base ship, only the shuttle-craft. But you've taken all the necessary precautions. Captain, you have everything well in hand."

"Yes, sir."

"Then I'll get to it, captain."

"Final orders, sir?"

"Yes."

Captain Ayla said "yes" under her breath and opened her tablet. "May I ask about the Lieutenant Halley situation, sir?"

"Why?"

"We're a soldier down, sir."

"Lieutenant Centaurus can fill in effectively."

"Sir, you and I have been at this a while. Putting together the right team for a mission is often hard enough, and most of the time you have to make do with what you have or don't have. This time, we had the time and resources to put together the right team. This is the Titan mission. We have to get it right."

"I remember when you first arrived aboard the Tyson, captain, as a junior scientist. Never did I think you had the mettle or inclination to rise to C.O. and captain the ship. Never thought you particularly even liked people, based on your background and psych evals, but you weren't to be messed with when it came to the science. I thought you'd be holed up in your lab forever. You didn't want it then but something changed along the way."

"It was one of the rotations one year, sir. I can't even remember if it was Navy or Army. Brand new officers wide-eyed, full of energy and expectations, nervous as well. They couldn't believe they were actually in space. One of them had a list of quotes from a book he culled from one of the many inspirational speeches the officers heard during graduation week in AIT. The only one he paid attention to. It said: 'In this vast, big universe, you have choices. You can be the star, the center of attention and master of the solar system; the planet, following after the star like a puppy dog; or the moon following the planet like a puppy dog. I prefer to be the star.' A day later, I got on the command track."

The Admiral squinted his eyes. "You're talking about me?"

Captain Ayla smiled. "Yes, sir. You were that one command officer he paid attention to. I actually made a copy of that ensign's list of quotes. Some good ones there, sir. And sir, I don't like people. But if I want to be a star, I need those planets and moons to follow me around. Scientists have egos too. I want Halley back. I spent years getting the right team for science services. I never thought I'd have the right one on the Army side but then came Halley and he radically changed things, sir. Not just for the better. For the best."

"Yes, I know what he did there."

"His predecessors were bums, sir. But I'm sure you know that, too. I want him back, sir. I know what he has to do, but I, we, want him back."

"I know you do, captain. I do, too. But for the time being that can't be helped."

"Sir, may I speak bluntly?"

"You always do, captain."

"'Approved leave of absence,' sir? You may be the boss of bosses to us, but even you report to someone. I can't imagine they'd be pleased with you."

"Captain, I actually have more bosses than there are sailors and soldiers on the Tyson. You don't even want to know. The situation isn't about the 'leave' but I can say no more."

"You want him to go to Uroboros, sir."

The Admiral said nothing. "Captain, let's get to your final orders."

"Yes, sir. I'm decrypting them now on my screen."

"The architects will arrive on Titan in a year."

"We'll have the moon to ourselves for six months then, sir," Ayala said as she quickly read the orders.

"The Marines will be there in seven months, one month after your touchdown."

"A platoon, sir?"

"You'll be getting a company, captain."

"A company, sir? Two hundred Marines?"

"Yes."

"Military services will outnumber science services. Is our fundamental mission changing, sir?"

"Scientists are still in charge, captain. You're just getting a lot more bodyguards."

"Should I read anything else into the situation, especially given what happened to the KCS Uji Kauboi, sir?"

"No. Ignore that mess. We have enough on our plate."

"Yes, sir."

"Captain, also don't get too locked into your final orders."

"Sir?"

"There may be changes."

"I should expect more final orders, sir? Final-final orders? Or final-final-final?"

"No need to get cheeky, captain. Nothing is out of the ordinary. Remember, we're making history as we go. None of us have ever done any of this before. Focus on the mission and ignore everything else."

"Yes, sir."

"Operation Fairy Dancer is finally here, captain, and there are a lot of excited people in Command and on Earth."

"I'm excited too, sir."

"Space explorers to real planet tamers."

"Yes, sir."

"I'll be in contact at the designated time marks. Good night, captain."

"Good night, sir."

His face disappeared from the screen. Ayala jumped up from her chair and ran to the door. It opened and an anxious Lieutenant Centaurus was already waiting, holding his tablet.

"What the hell is happening with the mission?" she said to him. "The Marines will be there one month after we touch down, and the architects just seven months later. We're supposed to have Titan for nine months before anyone shows up. What's happening to the mission?"

"What are they not telling us?" Lieutenant Centaurus asked.

"Ignore the KCS Uji Kauboi? How do you ignore the spacing of over one hundred military personnel by unknown hostiles, using the very same—but unsuccessful—tactics used against our own ship, and we had to blow up their ship in space?"

"Tell the others?"

"No! No. We need to process all of this. Keep it to ourselves for the moment."

Chapter Nine

588 Achilles-2

The second they got the message from the bridge that the civilian mining ship was en route, Halley got his gear and exited the temporary quarters he was assigned. His Navy counterpart on the Tyson anticipated his move, not his men, but here he'd be able to sneak away and send his goodbye by way of encrypted message as he flew to the Belt Colonies.

Nothing doing.

Lieutenant Hajime had Lieutenant Yi-so-yeon and the red uniforms at attention in the corridor to the launch bay. Halley, in his super-suit, with his helmet in his hand, couldn't suppress his grin. He walked up to the junior officer and stopped.

The greatest trait of a subordinate officer was the ability to anticipate a commanding officer's next action and needs. The junior officer was a natural and would go far in service. If the KCS didn't treat him right, NAA Command would take him.

"Lieutenant, one space soldier to another, you're going to be running the entire UROK armed forces in the future, aren't you?" Halley said to Hajime.

"Sir, it was an honor serving with you!" Lieutenant Hajime saluted and Lieutenant Yi-so-yeon and the red uniforms followed suit.

Halley saluted back. The Kauboi crew relaxed.

Halley moved to Lieutenant Yi-so-yeon. "Lieutenant, confidence comes with experience. You'll get both and then the stars are the limit for you, too. In the Americas, we'd say you were some smart, squared-away space soldiers. You kept your cool and did your duties. Your command won't forget it. I'll make sure of it."

Then Halley yelled, "Lieutenant, request permission to disembark!"

"Granted, sir!" Hajime responded.

#

The NCS Neil deGrasse Tyson had passed its halfway point—six months to Titan. However, Halley was headed in the opposite direction, to the MAB (Main Asteroid Belt) between Mars and Jupiter. Seven months to Jupiter and another ten to the Belt. The Tyson crew wanted to see him again but didn't ever expect to, or if they did, years later. Space travel was faster than it had been in the ancient space era but it was still a slow, steady slog to wherever you wanted to go past Mars. However, they didn't know about Nebula.

Besides the MAB, three other smaller asteroid belts rotated within Jupiter's orbit: Greek, Trojan, and Hilda—Jupiter's Trojan asteroids.   The number of asteroids in each cluster depended on how small one wanted to count. Asteroidal debris ranged from a small moon to pebbles, but the cut-off for a real "asteroid" was down to about a kilometer.

Halley flew straight for Jupiter's Greek asteroid swarm at maximum burn and then some. His "little" NCS Capricorn shuttle would earn its pay this trip. It was a lonely trip with only his auto-pilot on-board computer as company. He'd remain in his s-suit the whole trip. He could have engaged auto-pilot, but this was deep space. Alone, but with another hostile ship, and possibly a base ship of some kind out there in the expanse. Too many dangers, so Halley would stay awake and do the piloting himself.

This is Terran automated space beacon Delta. You are leaving Saturn Space and entering Jupiter Space.

The message came on his traffic comms over the pre-set English channel. Earth had over a thousand major languages and countless dialects on top of that, but in space there were only five recognized international languages.

588 Achilles was a large Jupiter Trojan asteroid in the Greek cluster. The eighty-three-mile-long D-type asteroid was the first Jupiter Trojan ever discovered, but Halley wasn't flying to it. He was flying to its "twin"— 588 Achilles Two. But the asteroid wasn't created by the cosmos or by God, based on your belief system. It was a top-secret joint creation of the USS Army and Marines almost a century ago and continuously upgraded over the years. If someone was watching from afar, they might wonder why the asteroid moved out of its orbit and at an abnormal speed all of a sudden.

Halley had turned off his engines and let inertia do all the work. Two bodies—his shuttle and the secret asteroid ship—floated to each other. It was pitch black outside, so he watched everything from the sensors screen.

Slowly, slowly. Bump. Click.

The ships were docked. His trained ears heard the suction seal and pressurizing.

Full-suited with his helmet on, Halley entered the docking bay and the rest of the ship. Sections of the corridors lit up dimly as he walked, then went dark as he moved past. The design was very much like Navy—sterile, all-white surfaces. He stopped in front of the main door to the ship's Control Room—a massive gray steel vault-like door hatch.

There was a blast of light from the ceiling and floors, then all went dark. He'd been scanned.

Lieutenant Joshua Halley. USS Army. Assigned to the North America Cosmoship Neal deGrasse Tyson. Identity confirmed. Access granted.

After the computer voice sounded, the control door opened and all the lights turned on as he stepped into the room.

Halley was startled and almost drew his weapons. A humanoid stood in the center of the barren room. As he watched the silver android take on more female characteristics, skin tone developed over its silver face and hands. Its eyes stared at him with a creepy, unnerving silvery tint. It was a holdover from times past when roboticists were obsessed with making androids as human-like as possible rather than robots that did the job that the military needed.

"Does my appearance disturb you?" the android asked.

Halley was annoyed. The machine had biometric sensors to "see" his conscious and sub-conscious physical reactions, as well as AI analytics to determine the emotional states of human beings.

"Please don't analyze me," Halley said. "I didn't know there was an android interface aboard. I need an emergency burn to the Belt Colonies."

"Nebula engine is powering up. Launch time is thirty-seven minutes from now."

"Are sensors active?"

"Sensors are active and fully functional."

"Do sensors detect any other ships in our region or flight path?"

"No ships detected other than the NCS deGrasse Tyson en route to Saturn, the KCS Uji Kauboi en route to the Belt Colonies, and the KCS Mining Ship Bolasaeg Hyeseong en route to the KCS Uji Kauboi."

"Good."

"May I query?"

"Yes."

"Is your intent to know of other vessels in the region besides the three named?"

"Yes, but you named all the ships on your sensors."

"Yes, but my sensors detect other possible life signs not affiliated with any of the three ships detected."

"Life signs. How would you detect life signs?"

"Through infrared or audio detection. My sensors detect possibly seventy-two life signs emanating from an orphan asteroid in our flight path's trajectory. Is that the information you wanted?"

"Yes, it is."

The android had likely found the hostiles' hidden base ship.

♦ ♦ ♦

The android activated the external view screens to see the computer CGI recreation of the asteroid where the life signs were coming from.

Halley stood next to "her" in full super-suit. He could have sworn that the machine was only about five feet, but he glanced briefly at it. She was now the same height as he was.

"Is it a real asteroid?" Halley asked, looking back at the screen.

"It is. Originally from Jupiter's Hilda asteroid cluster."

"Can we launch without it seeing us?"

"We technically cannot see it."

"But when we launch, we will be in its line of sight."

"I can calculate the optimum flight plan to avoid line of sight detection but not detection of our propulsion system. However, our burst would likely appear as an unexplainable anomaly on their sensors. The sun's rays will also hit us in sixteen minutes, which we can use to our advantage."

"Plot the course, then. Do we have weapons?"

"We have all standard weapons you are familiar

with.”

“Which means you have other weapons that I’m not authorized to use or know about?”

“That is correct.”

“Where do you need me to go until our launch?”

“There is a rest and relaxation room at the end of the hall. Full entertainment center. Fully stocked kitchen. For all food meals, simply add cold or hot water based on your preference.”

The android smiled at him.

At least he’d be in the MAB soon, within a stone’s throw of Uroboros.

Chapter Ten

Sightings

The Tyson bridge crew gathered around the screen table. Pvt. Superjovian had transferred the display there.

"What did you see?" Captain Ayla asked the commander.

Commander Cassiopeia looked up at the private for a second, then back at the table screen. "I'm sorry, captain, I thought I saw something show up on Titan."

Lieutenant Centaurus and the Sarge stood opposite the Commander and the doctor at the table screen.

"Is this a joke?" Lieutenant Centaurus asked.

"No, Lieutenant, this is not a joke. We scientists like to be precise."

"'I thought I saw something' doesn't sound too scientifically precise," the Lieutenant said.

"Captain, with everything going on, I wanted to at least bring it to your attention. I thought I saw a blip on the sensors for Titan."

"Commander, I have to side with the L.T. on this one. We're all on edge. We're as susceptible to the mind playing tricks on us as the soldiers are. Why were you even on Sensors?"

"The private had to go to the head."

"Anything to add, private?" Captain Ayla asked.

"I've been focusing all my sensor sweeps on threats to the ship, Cap," he replied.

"Cap? I'm not Captain America, Britain, or Canada. Ayla. It's only two syllables. It means 'halo' or 'moonlight.' You address me, private, as Captain Ayla or ma'am, Private Superjovian."

"Umm...ma'am, no one says my whole last name. I'm either Minotaur or Private Super."

The crew tried not to laugh. Ayla was clearly annoyed.

"Let's stick with Private, shall we?"

"Yes, ma'am."

"Simple enough remedy, commander. Get the tapes and we'll rewind and rewatch what was recorded."

"Exactly why I brought you back to the bridge, ma'am."

The captain walked to her station and began typing commands on the keyboard. Everything on a cosmoship was recorded, everything. All data was then stored digitally as well as hard-coded on data disks. Retrieving that recorded data was not as straightforward, which was by design.

Captain Ayala walked back to the screen table and pushed a button. "How far back am I rewinding?"

Commander Cassiopeia looked at the bridge clock. "Rewind ten minutes, ma'am."

The captain played the rewound screen recordings. They all saw the blip, which showed up for only a fraction of a second. The captain rewound by frames and stopped.

"Pull it up and do a full analysis."

"Yes, ma'am."

Everyone looked at the image on the screen table.

"Sarge?" the Lieutenant asked.

"Lieutenant, that looks like a ship," the Sarge replied.

"Ship?" Lieutenant McAuliffe asked.

"There's not supposed to be anyone else on Titan, Sarge," Pvt. Superjovian said nervously.

"Private, I said it looks like a ship. Doesn't mean it is. Could be anything," the Sarge said. "Could be a meteor, and we do have probe satellites around Titan. One could have crashed."

"If it helps you sleep, private, every inch of Titan has been viewed, watched, mapped, photographed, recorded, and digitized for almost five hundred years. Most of that activity has been in the last fifty years in preparation for our mission. It's not a ship, that I can tell you. We'll be the first humans on Titans," the captain said reassuringly, but even she realized her mistake.

"Humans, ma'am?" the private asked.

♦ ♦ ♦

"I'm sorry," Captain Ayala said to the Sarge.

The captain stepped into the briefing room with the LT and Sarge. This time, the Captain insisted that the doctor remain outside in the Control Room.

"Captain, we have a ship full of mostly young people with overactive imaginations who are gossiping about ships being blown up and people spaced. For some damn reason, they've gotten it into their minds about aliens. We don't need this. Identification of that blip is a priority."

"Of course, it's a priority. The Commander will handle it. If you're that worried, assign some of your soldiers to identify it, too."

"I like that," the Sarge said. "That'll give them something to do."

Then there was silence. They all looked at each other.

Ayala shook her head. "It isn't a ship. We're the only ones out here. You two are as bad as your soldiers."

"Can I play devil's advocate, captain?" the Lieutenant asked.

"No, because it's not a ship. Lieutenant Centaurus, how could another ship speed past us, get to Titan, and casually set up shop without us or anyone else in the Solar System, including Earth, seeing them? Who? What ship could do that? Who?"

"I don't know. You're right, captain. I'm just uneasy."

"Gentlemen, I need you to be calm and rational. We all need to be calm and rational. Let's not have the kids who are afraid of the monster under the bed, get the parents to start believing in monsters under the bed. Our only monsters to deal with are another possible hostile behind us, saying prayers for Halley and his father, and keeping this crew focused on the mission."

"Second that for Halley and his dad," the Sarge said.

"Third," the Lieutenant said.

"Besides, what do we have to fear? The Army is here. We get to Titan and you'll protect us all. Then the Marines arrive in a month."

"Captain, just be very careful how you speak in front of the crew," the Sarge said. "I had the same conversation with the L.T. here."

"Won't happen again, Sarge," Captain Ayala said. "Let's get out here before they think something's wrong."

◆ ◆ ◆

With his big seven-foot body, Private Superjovian had to recline in his chair to get comfortable at the Sensors station. At first he stood, but he couldn't stand his entire watch. The "quiet work," as soldiers called it, was the norm in Army life, and for all of the armed services for that matter. Like any good soldier, he was good at it. One learned all kinds of tricks to stay sharp while doing the mundane work—in this case, watching the sensors' data feeds and scopes like he had a dozen eyes. No one spoke aloud about it anymore, and even the whispering was gone, but everyone was still nervous. They were, after all, alone in deep space.

The commander appeared at his station. He was looking at her, but she was looking at his displays. "What are you tracking, private?"

"The Bogeyman, ma'am," he replied with a smile.

Commander Cassiopeia stepped closer. "Who authorized this?"

"I took the initiative, ma'am."

She folded her arms, thinking, not knowing whether to scold him.

"Should I tell you what I'm seeing, ma'am?"

"Private, you piqued my interest. Make sure you live up to the anticipation."

Captain Ayla had finally gotten her mind to settle down as she lay in bed. Hopefully, sleep would follow soon, but she just closed her eyes and didn't bother to expect it. Then the cabin doorbell sounded.

She slowly opened her eyes and rolled from her side to her back. "Yes!"

The door to her quarters opened. "Sorry, ma'am." Commander Cassiopeia stood at the doorway but wasn't alone.

"Come in, already."

"Ma'am?"

"I'm naked and I'm not shy. Get in here and close the door. The light in the hallway is bothering my eyes."

The commander stepped in with the private, Sarge, and the L.T.

"He was headed to Jupiter's Greek asteroid cluster at max burn, then vanished from sensors," said Private

Superjovian. The Sarge gave him a nasty look. "Ma'am," the private quickly added.

Capt. Ayla looked at the tablet sitting on her bed.

The private continued. "I kept a sensor group on the cluster to see if I could pick him up again. At zero-one-twenty-two hours, sensors observed one of the asteroids break from its orbit and head to MAB."

Ayla looked at L.T. and Sarge.

"Don't look at us," the L.T. said.

"So, Army does have a secret asteroid ship," Ayla said. "Interesting but could have waited until my watch started. We knew he wasn't going to fly his shuttle ten, eleven months to get to the MAB."

"Ma'am, that's not why we're here," the commander said.

"Ma'am, the asteroid ship, based on its speed, will reach the MAB in about a month," the private continued.

"A month?" the captain asked suspiciously. "You checked your calculations?"

"The computer did the calculations, ma'am," the private replied.

"Did you check the computer's work?"

"I did, ma'am. The commander checked my work. A month, ma'am. It's moving that fast. Faster than anything we've ever seen."

Ayla looked at Commander Cassiopeia with a smile. "They built it!" She looked at the private. "Do you have all the sensor data?"

"Yes, ma'am. I almost lost it but found it again. The computer is mis-cataloging the data. If it passed by, I don't think sensors would even know it was a ship."

"The Army built what?" Commander Cassiopeia asked.

"Yes, built what?" the Sarge asked.

"I notice the L.T. isn't surprised," Ayla said.

"I am surprised. Captain, I'm privy to the same publications you are. We're all in command, so we're all always looking for news or clues on the latest weapons, ships, and tech."

"They built the Nebula engine," Ayla answered.

"Nebula engine?" Cassiopeia asked.

"FTL is impossible, or until someone discovers a

way," Ayla said.

The private looked at everyone.

"Faster-than-light travel, private," Sarge added for him.

He smiled. "Cool," he said.

"Hyper-light might be impossible, but scientists believe that hypo-light speed in space is very much within our capability. That theoretically we can't break the light speed barrier, but we can reach any speed under it."

"We've been told the engine wouldn't be possible for another hundred years," Commander Cassiopeia said.

"We always knew that wasn't true," Ayala said. "Personally, I thought it was thirty to forty years away."

"Don't look at us," the Lieutenant said. "We know nothing about it."

"Lieutenant Centaurus, don't feel bad. I'm sure Navy is hiding all sorts of things from me, too."

"I'm sure Navy built it," Cassiopeia said to get a rise out of the men.

"Army all the way," Sarge said.

"Then why don't we have it on the Tyson, ma'am?" the private asked.

"Probably it's the next big press release. First Titan, then this Nebula," Captain Ayala said.

The Commander nodded. "Ma'am, I bet that's it. We build the colony first then we have the engine to get you there.'"

"Gotta love capitalistic greed. As long as it doesn't mess with my science, I'm fine with all of it," Ayla said.

"The next big thing after this big thing," the commander said.

"I thought Europa was being teed up to be the next big thing?" Sarge asked.

"How many off-Terran colonies in deep space can we have, Sarge? We don't even have enough people for Earth after the last global population implosion and we have Luna and Mars. Then Titan. I'm sure there will be a Europa but we'll all be stardust for at least a couple of centuries before that happens."

"You know what this means," the L.T. said to Ayla.

Ayla nodded. "He wasn't lying or telling us what we wanted to hear. He may get to Titan with us after all, when he does what he has to do."

M.A.B. SPACE

Chapter Eleven

The Belt Colonies

This is Terran automated space beacon Gamma. You are leaving Jupiter Space and entering Main Asteroid Belt Space.

Deep space was the domain of soldiers and scientists, even if the bosses were governments and multinational conglomerates. But they were all back on Earth, most rarely venturing into space themselves. However, before the "reign" of soldiers and scientists, another group had made real space exploration possible: the miners. Off-world space mining became where the real money was and money was what made the universe (or solar system) go 'round, even in their century.

Space mining turned into a great gold rush for Earth and gave the planet's military forces their new great mission as glorified bodyguards. Halley and most soldiers didn't mind it at all if that meant no more wars. In fact, with one exception, there hadn't been a war on the entire planet of Earth in almost a century, and no one in the military of any nation was complaining—as long as the existence of the armed services was assured and the paychecks and raises kept coming.

The great profits of space mining, especially from the MAB, allowed Earth to return to its original, age-old desire of space exploration for pure science. But soon it would enter the age of terraforming, then space colonization. Earth Command was grinning from ear-to-ear with the coming new missions for their soldiers, sailors, and Marines.

Contrary to popular imagery, the Main Asteroid Belt was mostly empty. Asteroids were spread out over such a large orbital area that collisions between them were rare. Almost a million of them had official names, and there were millions more depending on how small one wanted to count. When did an asteroid begin and a rock end, as both were the same? Over two hundred asteroids were larger than a hundred kilometers, and over a million had a diameter of one kilometer or more. But the total mass of MAB still accounted for only four percent of the Earth's moon.

The four largest asteroids were Ceres, Vesta, Pallas, and Hygiea, making up over sixty percent of MAB's total mass. Ceres alone made up approximately thirty-nine percent of that mass and had a diameter of about nine hundred and fifty kilometers. The other three largest asteroids in MAB had diameters of less than six hundred kilometers.

Halley piloted his NCS Capricorn to the American section of the MAB on Ceres. He'd been deep in thought the entire trip from the Jupiter Greek cluster. The Admiral granting him leave was a double-edged sword. Being "on leave" meant that he was equivalent to a civilian. His rank would mean nothing to MAB security and his normal access to systems would likely be restricted.

"Command, this is the NCS Capricorn. Requesting permission for docking," Halley announced into traffic comms.

"Capricorn, entry code received. Permission for docking granted."

"Command, received and understood. Beginning docking approach now."

The Belt Colonies were not really colonies. They were a network of mining bases constructed on the vast

Asteroid Belt between Mars and Jupiter. A specific nation or its multinational owned individual bases, each one regarded as sovereign soil of that country.

The augmented asteroid base of Ceres was the oldest of the American MAB colonies. Through retrofitting, the mass of the asteroid had almost doubled, including the main mining facilities and restricted quarters, the general colony, a separate military base and scientific research center, the space dock, and the private military and corporate command. Within the body of the asteroid were the hidden and restricted energy, life support, and anti-grav generation services. Ceres was a colony in the sense that it was self-sustaining, without the support of Earth, but it was for soldiers, scientists, and miners only. No space tourism here ever—that was for Luna and Mars.

Click, seal, and pressurized. A steady green light flashed on the cockpit display and he got up for the door. Anti-grav generators had been perfected in the MAB and many said that one day the need for gravity ring tech would be made obsolete. Then would come the ability to create anti-grav for smaller ships like his shuttle. However, like the Argonaut-class ships, the landing bay for the much larger asteroid bases was within the structure, so no floating. Fully clad in his super-suit, he walked as normal to the main doors and flipped the latch button.

As the door opened, about a dozen armed security guards in dark brown uniforms and field caps were waiting for him. Halley stepped out, saying nothing, but he took off his helmet.

"Lieutenant Halley," he said.

The guards gave him a once-over as they lowered their rifles.

"Anything to report, lieutenant?"

"No. Smooth space sailing all the way."

"May I ask, lieutenant, where you came from? Control said that first you weren't there and then there you were."

"Sorry, sir, but that's classified. In fact, I won't be staying long. I need to check in with your military base. Army or Marines here?"

"Neither. They were all called off base. The military base is being manned by us."

"Civilians?"

"Yes, civilians with military training."

"I didn't mean any offense. Tell me who I need to check in with and I'll be on my way."

"Lieutenant, where will you be on your way to?" asked another guard.

Halley began to talk but was cut off by another.

"—I know it's not the Uroboros Orbiting Station, because all flights there are strictly prohibited by order of all Mil-Sci."

"What happened there?" Halley asked.

"Lieutenant, they never tell us civilians anything," the first guard said.

"Not much different for us," Halley said. "No, I'm not headed there. I'll need transport to Mars ASAP, though."

"Lieutenant, have you been here before?"

"I have, so I know the way to the base."

"Everything is where you left it, then. Check in with the duty officer and relax a bit."

"Why? What are you about to tell me?"

"One-day quarantine."

"No, I have to go."

"Sorry, sir," the guard said with a smile. "Since where you came from is classified, you can't leave until you get a full med check and one-day quarantine, or the formal clearance by Ceres Medical."

Halley sighed.

"We tried to help you, sir."

"Yes, I know. How do I get to Ceres Medical?"

"We'll happily shuttle you there, sir. But mentally prepare yourself for our medical officer to respond to your request for exemption with a 'Hell no' with excessive profanity at the beginning and end of that phrase. Many an admiral has tried and failed with him."

"Tough case, is he?"

"He's a bastard. Hates the military. Think it has to do with an ex-wife."

◆ ◆ ◆

Ceres security was right about their base chief medical officer. Halley's ears were still ringing from the cursing rant that the base medical officer gave him. First, the medical officer demanded that he disclose what base ship he came from. Then he threatened to throw Halley in the brig. Then, when the medical officer realized his yelling was having no effect whatsoever on the soldier, he told Halley to get out of sick bay but with enough curse words to make even Marines blush. The man did indeed hate military.

Halley took the chewing out in stride because the medical doctor of any base or ship was the one person who could outrank an admiral or general. The magic word was "contamination." With that, one person could shut down everything. Technically, the lieutenant was from a "place unknown" and he could hide behind being a military officer on a classified operation for only so long. Strangely, the doctor ended up being far more lenient than he would have been if the places were reversed and they were back on the Tyson.

Bottom line: Stuck on Ceres for a day! But he had to get to Uroboros! He said all this to himself as he sat alone at a table with a drink in front of him. The Ceres bar in the general colony section was huge. On a cosmoship, space was at a premium, but the drinking bar and lounge seemed larger than those on Earth. However, it did make sense as there was no other bar on Ceres and there was little else to choose from in terms of recreation.

Halley realized that the reason why so few people were in the three-level bar was that it was between shifts. Ceres remained primarily a mining station and the miners were at work. No one drank before a shift. Even the dumbest of miners didn't do that. However, when the miners came off shift, they'd consume enough alcohol to make them comatose until the next day, when they'd start working again. Halley had never understood the life until he found out that the salary of an average miner was far, far greater than a soldier's. The flip-side of that was that, in the rare cases of a reported death in space, it was always a miner—never a soldier, sailor, or Marine.

He was able to accomplish at least one thing. Ceres security took him to the military base to check in but no personnel were there. As an active duty soldier, he didn't need to see a live person to get access to the locker and storage rooms to store his gear and s-suit, then dress in civilian clothes so he could at least pretend to blend in. He took the added step of wearing a knit cap to hide his military hairstyle. Fortunately, knit caps were common among civilians.

Architecture that did not have to concern itself with exteriors tended to be on the unimaginative side, as Terrans noted. Halley was always amazed by the colors, boldness, and fanciness of dwellings on Earth whenever he visited. But they had a planetary atmosphere. For off-worlders, they had cosmoships, biospheres, and space stations.

The giant bar was probably as creative as the owners could be, or cared to be. Bars all tended to look the same—counters with bartenders and a wall of booze behind them; barstools and tables for the boozers. Everything else was unnecessary. Lighting tended to be on the dimmer side and the music was always low, often "oldies." However, the next big attractions after alcohol were big screen displays playing vintage or current sports. That was what people wanted to see, whether they were on Ceres, Mars, Luna, or Earth. Real competitive sports could be played only on Earth. Maybe in the future that would change with a terraformed Titan.

Halley stopped drinking when a group came into the bar. The only civilians on Ceres were contractors to support military, science, or mining services. The new patrons who entered into the bar looked like civilian families—not tourists but, either way, they shouldn't be aboard an asteroid base. Moments later, a rush of loud miners coming off shift started packing into the bar. Most of them were still in their dirty red jumpsuit uniforms. Halley could determine who did what based on the amount of dirt and grime on their faces and uniforms: surveyors and mappers, excavators, loaders, drivers and haulers, and reconstructors. Management never joined the workers in recreation, per regulation, as the Company wanted a hard line between personnel and management, so neither side got too friendly. Management's job wasn't to meet a quota but to keep personnel alive.

The group of civilians did not consist of random visitors. Ceres miners were expecting them. Ignoring the TV sports, the miners quickly got their drinks and then gathered around them. From the corner of his eye, Halley noticed a couple of men enter in civilian clothes. One of them was among the Ceres security guards who greeted him.

"Why should the capitalists have full dominion over all the seas of space and its islands of planets and moons?" said the man Halley would learn was called Savior to the enraptured crowd of miners and bar employees. The man looked like some proverbial Jesus-like figure, with long hair to his shoulders, a mustache and beard. The man even wore a cloak, which Halley didn't think people anywhere wore anymore. "They get to seize the other planets of Sol and their moons. The first step in their conquest is Titan, but it won't be the last. They'll capture Saturn's great moon and dictate its government, dictate its laws, dictate who can or can't go there. Homesteaders view this as cosmic blasphemy. If this is a conquest for humanity, then all humans should be involved in the decisions and colonizations of other worlds, not the select few militaristic multinationals that seek to control other planets as they do with Earth.

"We will make our own claim for Titan, and we do not need the permission of any government or army. Join us. Join the Homesteaders as we colonize Titan and create our own destiny." The man paused and smiled wide. "Free of charge."

The crowd erupted in laughter and applause. Halley couldn't help himself.

"What you said is just plain reckless and stupid," Halley said, standing from his table.

"A challenge! Who, may I ask, are you?"

"Who I am is irrelevant."

"I am Savior."

"Are you now? Listen good, civilian. The reason that multinationals and governments are terraforming and colonizing Titan is because they have the money and you don't. What is that money doing? It's buying the expertise needed to make it all a reality. Do you know how to terraform a planet or moon? Build a biosphere? Build a ship or space engine? Do you even know how to repair an engine? Do you know how to power a colony 1.2 billion clicks from Earth? How about feed its population? And I mean grow real food, not meal packs you brought over from Earth. What about air and water? Do you know how to extract them from the atmosphere and ground? What about waste management? Space becomes a whole lot less fun when you're standing in a river of sewage. Do you know how to build a communication network so you can contact the rest of humanity? What about defenses? Meteors can crash into deep space moons too. Luna had to blast one of them out of space just last year that was coming its way. What about cosmic rays? Can you keep your colony shielded from them? Rays so powerful they can fry the systems of our best ships if they didn't have proper shielding. Imagine, what that could do to a human brain.

"Look around at all the men and women in this bar. Not one of them is merely a bar employee or miner. Every one of them is a proven space dweller. Any one of them could pass any psych eval you could throw at them, and has, and any one of them I could trust with my life. Space exploration is a lot more than hopping into a spaceship from Earth. And you want to live on another planetary body?

"Listen good, Mr. Savior. Take your people back home to Earth and do your homesteading there. Deep space isn't for stupid people."

Halley sat back down at his table.

To say one could hear a pin drop in the cavernous three-story bar would be an understatement. The crowd of miners began to disperse. Some headed to the exits and to their quarters; other decided to stay to drink and watch a game on the big screens.

Halley glanced up at the Homesteaders. Savior glared back with squinting eyes that could kill. His followers said something to him and he slowly turned away. They all left the bar, too.

Halley turned slightly and could see the two security guards in civilian clothes begin to leave as well. The one he recognized gave him a "thumbs up" sign.

♦ ♦ ♦

Halley ran out of the bar after the two Ceres security men. "Can I walk with you, gentlemen?"

"Of course, lieutenant," answered the one he knew.

"When did our deep space bases start allowing civilians?"

"There are no regulations saying we can bar them. They arrived. We had to let them dock. The general colony is just that—open to the general public."

"Ceres Station is a secure mining base."

"Ceres Station has restricted and unrestricted areas, and always has."

"Are you telling me that civilians are flying around space now?" Halley asked.

The guards stopped. "Sir, I'll say this to you off-the-record, because even though your full ID file is blocked, we know you're part of the Titan project. You have no idea of all the things that have been happening in the inner colonies, here, and back on Earth."

"Like what?"

"That's all I'm going to say, sir. Also, I wouldn't tell anyone that you're military. I mean that."

"Hold on a minute. Then can you get me the latest intel files on Uroboros?"

"Sir, absolutely not."

"Why not?"

"Why not? Because I'd be fired, thrown in the brig, or both. You did notice that none of your military colleagues are here, right?"

"Why aren't they already there?"

The two security guards stared at him. "You tell us. They ran out of here like they were on fire and launched out the bay but not in the space station's direction."

"Okay, I'm going to tell you a secret, but it's only between us."

"Classified secret, sir?"

"No. Personal secret. I need to get to Uroboros because my father was aboard."

"Sorry to hear that, sir. Military too?"

"Part of the tech staff."

"Sorry."

"All I know is that no bodies have been found, so there's hope, but I need to get there."

"Whatever happened, sir, you're not going to be able

to do anything about it. It's too late."

"But there's a chance. I just have to be there. See for myself."

"I understand, sir. But our hands are tied. We can't even let you have your ship back until your one-day quarantine is over."

"Some quarantine. I was just in the base mega-bar with every miner from an entire shift."

"Yes, sir. The quarantine is bullshit but rules are the rules, even if they make no damn sense."

"I just need to get there."

"Too risky, sir. Wait for your soldiers to return."

"I guess I'll have to."

"I'm sure those Homesteaders will be leaving anytime now, after the shutdown you gave them."

Halley looked at the crowd of them walking away down the corridor. "How many ships do they have?"

"The Homesteaders might not know much about surviving in space and all the things you said, but it seems they do know how to build a decent cosmoship."

"They built them?"

"Built each one themselves. Cosmoships with big guns," the other security guard added.

♦ ♦ ♦

The landing bay of the Ceres had a massive observation deck. All non-military ships could be seen from the comfort of a thick glass or on the wall screens. Halley stared at the Homesteader ships. All he could think of was how ridiculous their external design was and how only people who grew up on fiction TV would build them. True deep space exploration demanded simple ships with functionality and safety in mind. The Homesteader ships displayed neither. They looked like giant starfish with lots of fins and even though they did have big rail guns, their placement seemed more as an afterthought than the natural design of the ship. If he were to see one in space, he'd hardly be impressed. "Amateurish" was what they said to him but beggars couldn't be choosy, as the saying went.

He found one of them in a different part of the bar. Where else could the civilians go on Ceres? His personal introduction was quick and he went straight to the point.

"You want a ride?" the man asked incredulously.

"You don't even do that back on Earth. Hitchhiking."

"I need to get to Uroborous Station."

"What's that?"

"One of the orbital stations in MAB."

"Don't you have your own ship for that? Can't be far if we're in the asteroid belt."

"For non-civilians, it's temporarily restricted."

"But not for civilians?"

"Correct."

"Still illegal."

"Not for civilians."

"Seems curious that a man as smart as you needs stupid people to get to a station he could almost walk to."

"It's a little farther away than a walk. And I said what I said because I don't think there's anything smart about dying a horrible death in space."

"We don't disagree."

"I can pay."

"Homesteaders take care of each other. All our needs are met."

"Very utopian of you, but out here people use money."

"You're a very closed-minded person."

"Idealism doesn't work well out here in deep space. And I've been a space explorer for my entire adult life, so I couldn't be that close-minded."

"Tell you what. Ask Savior. If he says it's okay, I'll take you to this Uroboros."

"Sounds fair enough. Where do I find him?"

"He's walking to us."

Halley turned around slightly. The man was approaching with several others.

◆ ◆ ◆

He sat down, never taking his eye off Halley. The others with him—five men and two women—grabbed chairs from surrounding tables to pull to the table and sit down around them. They were back in the bar, which was now very packed and noisy.

"Savior, this man wants me to take him to another station in the Asteroid Belt. Says it's restricted for non-civilians but not us. I told him to ask you. Ironic that a smart man needs a stupid man to help him out."

"Don't you know hitchhiking is dangerous?" one of the women said to him.

"I just need to get down the road. Not far."

"Why?" Savior asked. "I got the notion that you were offended by my talk."

"I was offended by your use of the word 'blasphemy.'"

"Why is that?"

"Ever met one of the Soul of Earth disciples? They believe you and I are blasphemers for exploring space. They believe humanity must remain on Earth. That we're cosmically linked, our souls are, in fact, one. To them, leaving Earth is akin to killing Mother Earth and to do so would mean the very end of humanity. Space exploration of any kind is killing the Earth and ourselves.

"How do we know they're wrong? We haven't been living in space long. When we colonize Titan, who knows what long-term separation will do to those living there? Maybe nothing, maybe something profound we can't even fathom today. What I'd say to them is that I don't know and neither do they. I hate when people speak with such certainty when, in fact, they know as little as I do about the universe."

Savior's anger had lessened but not his attitude. "Why do you need to get there?" he asked again.

"I just need to."

"We need to get to Titan. So, we came with ships to get there. If you need to get to this station, you should have brought your own ship."

"You're absolutely right. Actually, I did. Then I found out it's restricted to non-civilians."

"So, you wish to circumvent the law?"

"I need to get there, not debate it." Halley stood from the table.

"You give up too quickly."

"I never give up. I just don't waste time with things that can't get me where I need to go."

"You're military, aren't you?"

"I am."

"How much did he say he'd pay you?" Savior asked his man.

"He didn't say. He only insulted our communal way of life."

"I did no such thing. What do you think the military is?"

"How much will you pay us?" Savior asked.

"Pay us? I'll pay whoever can take me to the station, right now."

"We'll take you then but not for money."

"For what, then?"

"Knowledge. You were right. We don't know a thing about colonizing a new world. But you do. We don't know the questions to ask."

"Take me there right now and I'll tell you all the questions you need to ask and get answered."

Savior stood and extended his hand. "We have a deal, then."

Halley shook his hand but his gut was still uneasy about the man.

Chapter Twelve

Uroboros Space Station

alley marched into the Ceres general landing bay fully clad in his super-suit. The waiting Homesteaders stared at him nervously—Savior and a lot more of them than he thought were aboard. He knew he looked like some kind of killing cyborg even without his helmet.

"That's a military suit," Savior said as Halley stopped and towered over them.

"Shall we leave?" Halley asked.

"We're ready now."

Halley scanned the crowd. "All of you?"

"We left Earth together and we travel everywhere together as a people in space and beyond, even to drop off a hitchhiking soldier."

Once aboard, he studied the corridors and inner layout as they led him to the cockpit. He might have laughed at the exterior of the ships, but inside was the opposite. For a cosmoship built by civilians, it conveyed solid construction with a simple, functional design. Halley reasoned that two different teams built their ships—the "adults" did the interior and the "children" built the outside.

"Admiring our shipbuilding?" Savior asked him as they reached the cockpit section. "We may not know all the things you say we should, but we can build space vessels. We should. Between all of us, we have five hundred years of cosmoship construction at Pearl Harbor Spaceship Yards. Thirty of that from me alone."

Halley nodded. So, the Homesteaders could build a decent spaceship.

The cockpit of their ship was similar in function to that of a Nautilus-style C and C. Navigation and helm duties were shared by three people. Behind it all were passenger seats where Halley sat quietly as the Homesteader crew launched. Savior, of course, was the captain and planted himself in the conn chair.

"Take her out, Mr. Jeremiah," he called out.

"Launching Exodus One, sir," one of the men at the helm responded.

"Sir, we have a message from the Federation," a woman on communications said.

Halley couldn't see Savior's face but imagined his expression. He could see the face of the woman, who expressed surprise. Her eyes darted to her captain, and then she looked away, pretending to not have said what she did.

The Federation?

Halley fastened his helmet over his head. The action made more than one member of the Exodus One crew look at him. However, Savior never turned around in his chair.

Now things were beginning to make sense. Space exploration was neither simple nor cheap. The Federation was funding the Homesteaders. Halley stored the information in the back of his mind.   Right now, he had other priorities.

◆ ◆ ◆

Earth had ten orbiting space stations, Luna had one, and Mars had three. Orbital stations were for either pure scientific research or space tourism. However, none of the Sol stations were like Uroboros; she alone orbited the MAB.

When it was first commissioned over a century ago, it was the most important station in the solar system because, at the time, it had the sensors to precisely map an asteroid for every speck of precious ore to be found. Back then, space military made no pretense that they were anything more than highly-paid—and extremely dangerous—bodyguards for a commercial enterprise. The Uroboros Station made Planet Tamers MN the global power it was today. However, the once state-of-the-art sensor tech was now standard on any cosmoship that left Earth.

Uroboros was reclaimed by the scientists and it became the chief research station for the science of the origin and evolution of the universe—cosmology. People still thought it was the study of cosmetics, even in the age of space travel. For the medical scientific community, Uroboros was the primary research center for the effect of cosmic rays on the human body and brain.

The orbital space station was home to a hundred

people—mostly scientists, a small tech crew, and an even smaller military presence. In the past, it had been a truly international base but over the decades had become more and more dominated by the Americas. Sensors said that no one was aboard the entire station and all hails by the Exodus One's comm officer were unanswered. Uroboros was a floating gravity-ringed cylinder in space on auto-pilot.

Halley had been fighting the utter feeling of helplessness about the situation, though military were far from helpless beings. One thing after another delayed his getting to Uroboros, but in deep space, everything moved at a snail's pace. No matter how quickly you wanted things to happen, slow and steady was the nature of life and work in space. However, finally, the space station could be seen out the Exodus main observation window, though it was a floating derelict.

When Halley announced what he wanted to do, the bridge crew stared at him.

"I know your super-suits can do anything but do a spacewalk without a tether," Savior said to him. "We do know how to dock a ship."

Halley shook his head. "I want you out of here. We don't know what happened and I don't want your crew in any danger. You have families aboard. For all we know, someone could be waiting for someone to do just that. You can't fire those big guns of yours if you're docked with the station. I'll be fine."

"All alone on that station?"

"I won't be alone for long. Let me out of an airlock and get your ship out of the vicinity."

"What do you think happened to them?" one of the crew asked.

"I have no idea," Halley replied. "But I'll find out."

Savior rose from the conn. "Then let's get you on your way."

With several of his people, Savior escorted Halley to the landing bay section. They quickly reached a secure airlock where several guards were posted.

"I don't want you to draw any conclusions about what you heard before," Savior said.

"The Federation?"

Savior smirked. "Homesteaders are not part of the Federation."

"They just financed the trip."

"We see nothing wrong with the arrangement."

"Be careful with them."

"They say the same thing about Earth Command."

Halley grinned. "I'm sure they do."

"Not that we expect a favor."

"All this charity was to get me on your side?"

"No. For you to know of us. That's all. You know our names, you've seen our faces. We're not strangers anymore."

"Might come in handy in the future."

"That's what we're hoping."

"I'd say go back to Earth again, but I know I'd be wasting the words."

"I hope you find your father, Halley."

"Thank you, sir. I intend to."

The men shook hands. Halley fastened his helmet

and then he was in the airlock.

♦ ♦ ♦

Halley floated away from Exodus One into the darkness. The military spent many hours training its personnel in spacewalking, though few would ever use what they mastered in training in their entire career. Spacewalks just weren't done anymore—tethered or untethered. That was what bots were for.

The dark of space was temporarily gone as the Exodus engulfed him in lights to shine his way forward. Halley waved them on and gave them a "thumbs up" signal. The lights cut off and he could see the Exodus pull away. The vessel was returning to Ceres.

In the minds of many, spacewalking was the same as being spaced. A military super-suit was one of the most advanced pieces of tech ever made—robotic exoskeleton, offensive weapons, independent propulsion, life support, communications, sensors, defensive countermeasures. But even within the protection of his s-suit he felt utterly insignificant against the blackness of space. He wasn't the first and wouldn't be the last to ponder its limitlessness. The poet, intellectual, religionist, and astronomer could all stare at the entity of the cosmos for hours and never be at a loss for words or thoughts. Finally, Halley grabbed an outer handhold to the Uroboros Station, with only the light from his helmet to guide his way. He had arrived at last.

Had the admiral not given him the codes, Halley could still have gotten into the orbital station, even if he had to punch his way through the hull, which his s-suit had the power to do after a bit of time. But he had the codes to enter the empty space habitat circling the sun within the MAB on auto-pilot. Most people didn't know that Uroboros belonged to Planet Tamers MN. They had purchased it outright from the government years ago. The lieutenant was a commanding officer in the USS Army and an employee of the Company. He was through the emergency airlock and standing on the auxiliary lower deck with the gravity magnetic lock of his boots. Once, he exited the deck the gravity would kick in.

Lights were on and his suit indicated that life support was fully functioning. No warning lights or alarms. Nothing indicated that anything was amiss on the station at all, except that not a single person was aboard. Halley slowly marched from one level of corridors to the next, headed for the command deck.

He held a medium pistol, pointing at the floor as he moved. On his helmet's view screen was a small display from his rear helmet camera. On another was the feed from his suit's cam drone. The tiny hummingbird-sized drone flew ahead of him around corners and down the corridors. Even he was a bit unnerved by the eerie silence of the station. Nearly one hundred crew were gone without any indication that they had ever been aboard. Nothing out of place, no sign of struggle, but also no sign of violence, including blood, which was the only good thing.

For ages, the "Roanoake Scenario"—coming across a ship or station adrift where literally everyone aboard was gone—had been part of combat training for officers and enlisted. The simulation unnerved him then, even though he knew it wasn't real and there wasn't any chance of getting injured or killed. Psychologically, it was one of a human being's deepest fears—not knowing what happened.

This real version was no less unsettling. He could speculate forever, with each possibility more probable than the last. But it was still unknown. Whatever happened, he had to follow protocol, inspect the station, assess the observations and data, and piece together the sequence of events as best one could with or without corroborating evidence or logs.

Halley's audio was on the highest sensitivity. If anyone else was on the station, he could have heard their heartbeat. His scout drone ahead of him, he moved more quickly. With the final leap, he landed on the command deck. Not a soul in sight. A true ghost ship. He opened the door and entered the C and C. As Halley scanned the bridge, he was struck by how neat and orderly everything was. Not even a stray coffee cup on the conn.

The configuration of the bridge was command, navigation, helm, and tactical, all connected. In five minutes, he had every camera feed on the bridges active and showing him the mess hall, crew's quarters, labs, engines, cargo, hydroponics garden, life support and waste management, docking bay, power, communication, maintenance, astronomy, entertainment center, gym, sick bay, and chaplain/counseling. Not the most spacious of space stations but it had everything a rotating crew needed to live comfortably. In another five minutes, he had every external feed of the station on the wall screens.

However, sensors and comms were purposely down. Finally, a sign of something amiss. Then he saw the blip appear on Sensors. The second he saw the Barracuda-class shuttle appear on screen, dropping out of max burn and slamming to a stop, Halley deactivated the mag-lock of his boots and activated his s-suits own back thrusters to fly.

On the screen, he saw the first one, then followed by two more Space Marines. His audios heard them enter three different emergency air locks from the fore-section of the station. Three human rockets sped down the corridor to the bridge and the three Space Marines, in their dreadnought s-suits, banked around the corner just as Halley slammed the door to his escape pod on the bridge.

Thud!

The Marine struck the hatch in disgust and Halley heard an accompanying curse word in his audios. He'd escaped the Marines' combat ingress by split seconds. Now, all Halley had to do was push the launch button, but that wasn't what he wanted. Outside, they could shoot the pod out of space with their Barracuda and his own armored s-suit wouldn't have mattered. The Marines always got the best weapons and tech before Army or Navy. He still didn't know how they'd gotten through the station's hull so fast, as if they'd passed through walls. He was certain Marines didn't have molecular transfiguration tech yet but whenever it was invented, they'd get it first. He'd managed to get out of their clutches—but barely. And three angry Space Marines waited less than a few feet outside his pod.

◆ ◆ ◆

Halley didn't need to say or do anything. He just had to wait. If they knew he was aboard with sensors and could fly directly to his exact pinpoint location on the station, it wouldn't take them long.

"Lieutenant J. Halley, USS Army! Please step out of the pod," one of the Space Marine's voices boomed.

The lieutenant opened the pod's hatch and slowly exited. He stood tall at seven feet. Compared to unsuited humans, he looked like a killer robot. Next to the three Marines, he looked like a walking metal toothpick. They stood at least six inches taller but what made their combat s-suits so fearsome was the breadth. They were almost as wide as they were tall. The arms and legs of their suits were double the size of Halley's.

He couldn't stop himself from doing the "officer thing." He looked at the rank on their collar panels. All three were corporals, which meant, for the Marines, they weren't newbies and were the same as a veteran.

"Nice to meet you, Marines."

"Yes, lieutenant. You outrank us," said one of them with attitude.

"So? What I was about to say next Marine, is that we have work to do ASAP. Station comms and sensors have been fried, so that's the work. Comms and sensors. No delay. Do you disagree?"

"No, sir."

"Then let's hop to it. I'm sure you have the equipment on that advance ship of yours. Two on comms and two on sensors. Who does what, corporals?"

One of the Space Marines looked at the others. He pointed to one. "We'll do comms."

"Then we'll do sensors. I'll let you fly ahead of me since you have the combat back jets and Army gets the second-hand, third-rate crap back jets as always."

This was when no matter what branch of service one was dealing with, the military training kicked in. Everyone knew what to do and they went about it. Halley and the one Marine corporal worked exclusively on the bridge. All the sensor components had to be replaced. Whatever was used to make them inoperable had to have been fast and was definitely effective. The other two Marines flew to their attack ship once and spent most of their time outside the station replacing all the comm tower components and circuits. There was no chit-chat, just steady, quick work.

When the two Space Marines on comms returned to the bridge, sensors were back online. Halley and the Sensors Marine were quickly calibrated and tested everything. Soon, on display at the Sensor table, were every ship, station, asteroid, bot, and rock within three AUs (astronomical units) of Uroboros—two hundred and seventy-nine million miles in every direction.

The other two Marines didn't need instruction, either.

"Command, this is Team Lima-India-Oscar-November. Location secured. Target acquired," one of the Marines said into the comm station.

"So I've been 'acquired' have I?" Halley said to them.

"Team LION always gets their prey, sir," the Marine told him.

Halley unfastened his helmet and took it off. "Since we all know we're the real deal, no need for these." He hooked and fastened his helmet to his s-suits shoulder.

The other three Marines did the same but they all looked funny with tiny human heads on bulky metalloid bodies.

"Team LION, this is Command. Is Lieutenant Halley standing by?" a familiar voice asked over the comms.

"Command, he's right here," one of the Marines replied.

"Admiral, is that you?" Halley asked, stepping to the comm mic.

"Yes, it is, Lieutenant. Activating view screen."

Admiral Antares' face appeared first but it wasn't alone. Screen after screen activated with a different face, some in military uniform, others in civilian suits. Row after row, column after column of faces. Halley and the Marines were taken aback. They knew who they were looking at but not just Earth Command—the military and civilian political leadership of Earth Alliance.

"I have a question for you, Lieutenant," Antares said over the view screen.

"Yes, sir."

"As of now, One-Three Hundred Hours, you are

officially Captain Halley. Is that understood, soldier?"

Halley sighed. "Yes, sir."

"Is getting promoted a bad thing in the Army?" one of the Marines asked him under his breath.

"Now that we have that settled, report," the admiral said.

"Sir, before I answer that, may I know who these specimens of Marine humanity are standing on the station with me?"

"They are Corporals Fuller, Pei, and Suess," the admiral answered.

"Who do they report to, sir?"

"That would be me." Halley had never seen an actual general before but Gen. Nowlan of the USS Marines answered him.

"No, sir. Who do they directly report to?"

"That would be me, Captain. Major Tycho." The man's stern face looked suspiciously at Halley.

"Well, sir. I don't know what they're feeding you Marines these days, but in all my time, in all my training, never did I see a faster combat ingress of an unknown ship in my life. Time from your Barracuda outside the station to the bridge inside had to have been under two minutes. The only reason I escaped them snatching me from my escape pod was that I happened to be looking at the external cams, saw them, and said, 'Marines! Hide!' Impressive, sir."

There was a brief moment of collective laughing from the three Marines next to them and the Command staff on the view screens.

The Major chuckled. "Glad my men were able to get your heart pumping a little bit above normal."

Halley turned his attention back to the Admiral. "Here's what we know, sir."

Capt. Halley was thorough in his briefing. The Uroboros had been secretly boarded by unknown forces that took the crew and destroyed all sensor and comm logs. The erasure of the logs and the presence of all escape pods and spacecraft was the proof. Also, the fact that neither alert status nor weapons had been activated meant that whatever happened was fast and had incapacitated the crew before they could respond or defend themselves. Such a thing was unthinkable but Command agreed with his assessment.

"We've repaired all damaged systems so the station

is back to full operational status," Halley added.

"What are your recommendations, captain?" the admiral asked.

"We need any intel you have, sir."

"You'll have it."

"Will the NCS Konstantin Rokossovsky be rendevousing with us, sir?"

"The Marines aren't from the Rokossovsky."

"Sir?" Halley asked with a hint of confusion.

"Actually, the NCS Nicolaus Copernicus is en route to you."

"The Copernicus, sir? With the genesis architects?"

"Yes, captain."

"But that's a year ahead of schedule then, sir."

"That's affirmative, captain."

Halley took the cues from the admiral's face to stop asking questions.

"And the missing crew, sir?"

"The Marines will take charge."

"Then the Marines and I will await the Copernicus, sir."

"Good. You're in charge of the Uroboros until they arrive, captain."

"Yes, sir."

"Enjoy your brief respite, gentlemen. Over and out."

The faces of Command disappeared from the view screens.

Halley looked at the Marines. "Things are back to normal, then. Now we do what military does best. We wait."

♦ ♦ ♦

Halley didn't want the men separated at any time. There were still many unanswered questions so they waited in C and C with the main doors closed and locked. Two would stand watch on Sensors, and two would relax, which in this case involved a casual game of cards between two Marines.

"Sir, you can get some shut-eye while we man the stations," one of the Marines said.

"No, it's okay, corporal. Couldn't even if I wanted.

The Uroboros is a simple space station, but how do you get the drop on a hundred people?"

"Not that difficult, sir. Only a small fraction of them would be on duty at any time."

"Not one person could hit the alarm or automated distress call. No, this is something we haven't seen before."

"Sir." The Marine at the control stations gestured for him to come over. Halley joined him and saw that files were downloading.

"What are those files?" Halley asked him.

"The station's logs, sir."

"But they were fried. Physically destroyed."

"All stations have redundancies for rare situations such as this, sir."

"Copies of those logs are coming in. Copies that the station didn't know were being made."

"Every log made is automatically transmitted to an external relay on the hour, sir. Station crew doesn't need to know about it. This is military, not civilian, sir."

It was Captain Ayla who had told Halley, years ago,

that such a backup system had to exist on every cosmoship, transport, and station in the Sol system.

"Do we have the cams?"

The Marine looked up from his display. "Yes, sir."

"I don't care about anything else but those vid recordings. Start putting them up on the display. A different day and shift for each screen until we find what we're looking for."

"We know the day and time, sir."

The Marine started playing the first recording on the main screen of the bridge. It was a month ago and Halley's stomach sank. His father! The man on the bridge talking with the station's captain and XO looked like an older version of Halley. Judging from the tool bag in his hands, Halley's father had finished some kind of work. A crew of four young techs was with him. All the techs were in gray jumpsuits. Halley and the Marines watched the men talking and joking. Suddenly, they all stopped and dropped to the ground. Every crew member lay on the floor unconscious, a couple of them falling off their chairs.

Almost thirty minutes elapsed before the doors opened and there they were. None of them had ever seen the sparkling copper-colored exo-suits the intruders wore. There were no insignia or symbols to reveal what country or company they belonged to.

"Have you ever seen those kind of s-suits before?" Halley asked the Marines.

"No, sir," they said.

"Anything similar? Any clue as to who they are?"

"Not a clue, sir," one replied.

What was clear was that the intruder boarding party was huge. Soldiers kept coming through the doors. Crews went to all the stations, obviously to try to access systems, which would fail. But none of them seemed the least bit concerned. New soldiers entered the C and C with anti-grav trolleys, and they stacked the unconscious bodies on them like they were containers. Then they pushed their abductees out of the command room into the corridor.

One of the intruders looked at one of the cams and waved. He exited the room and was gone.

Halley flashed an angry look at the Marines.

"No need to say it, sir. You want to know who they are and exactly where they went. We'll put together a briefing for you."

♦ ♦ ♦

Halley sat on the floor just outside the main door to C and C, his eyes closed and his head dropped down, chin to chest. The Marines were poring over the video feeds and sensor logs. Anything he did would be more hindrance and annoyance, so he stayed out of their way.

The second he got the call from the Admiral back on the Tyson, he knew that whatever had happened on the Uroboros had taken place hours, or as much as a day and a half, earlier. Halley was a rescue operation, period. Halley wanted to find his father and the Uroboros crew badly and to "deal" with the persons responsible for the outrage. He didn't need to see the story the media would spin on every broadcast. It was the largest hostile act on a space station in Sol history. But then, he'd just come from another bit of history, or infamy: the largest death toll in space in Sol history.

"Sir, we got it for you," said one of the Marines.

Halley jumped to his feet and joined them at the command stations. On all the view screens were paused sample clips of different video feeds.

"Sir, we estimate there were at least sixty hostiles on board the Uroboros at any given time. Outside the station there may have been anywhere from ten to as many as fifty more of them.

"Where's their ship?" Halley asked.

"Sir, they got a stealth tech we've never encountered before. That and they knew exactly where to hold in space so they were basically in the blind spots of the external cams."

"There aren't supposed to be any blind spots."

"If the cams don't see anything, sir, they stay put. Nothing for them to focus on so they wouldn't move."

"The Uroboros crew?"

"They took them off the station, and we know they loaded them onto a smaller ship, but…"

"Not visible?"

"Correct, sir."

"Someone has real cloaking technology, then."

"Everyone's been working on it for decades, sir," said another Marine. "We thought we were close, but this makes ours look like we're throwing a wet blanket over our ships and yelling to people: 'Pretend you don't see anything.'"

"Marines are close, huh? You wouldn't mind elaborating with your Army brother from another mother, would you, Marine?"

"Nice try, sir, but that's—"

"Classified, yes. Big surprise."

"You mind telling us, sir, how the Army's commanding officer of the NCS Neil deGrasse Tyson is standing in front of us when he should be standing on said ship and we know he was on said ship a month ago? How'd you get to the MAB so fast, sir. Is Army hiding some new fangled engine from the military family, sir?"

"That's—"

"Classified," the Marine finished for him.

"What was their mission then, Marines, these intruders?" Halley asked.

"They were very deliberate about taking the crew, but we can't imagine that was their real mission. They destroyed the logs."

"How?"

"We don't know the method they used to fry the logs, sir. Whatever they used was fast and powerful. You saw the circuits. It was like they were hit point-blank by a concentrated solar flare without any shielding."

"Sir, we have no idea why they did what they did."

"Then my last question is where did they go in their cloaked ship or ships?" Halley asked. "I know you have something for me."

The Marines grinned at each other.

"Sir, yes, we do. Their cloak is very good but...you might not be able to see it with your eyes or sensors, but if it's not there, you should be able to see through it, like the stars, sir."

"A blank spot?"

"More like a distortion field, sir, like in an atmosphere when a jet is throttling its engines on the ground. The exhaust from its engine."

"Marine, tell me you plotted where they went."

"We have another something that doesn't make sense, sir. They weren't headed to known space."

Halley gave him a puzzled look.

"They were headed to wild space, sir."

Chapter Thirteen

Wild Space

In the early days of sea exploration, sailors thought that if a ship sailed too far, it would fall off the edge of the Earth. In Pre-Galileo times, humanity believed the Earth was the center of the universe, with the sun, planets, and everything else orbiting around it. In less than a millennium, humanity went from being the center of the universe to an insignificant speck in the cosmos.

But Wild Space, the common term, was like an old Terran sailing off a bottomless oceanic cliff into the unknown. In the modern Sol System, it was "all about circles." Space explorers never went outside the orbital circles of the planets. For decades, the outer boundary had been Mars. Then the space mining "gold rush" began. The MAB became humanity's outer edge in the quest for carbonaceous, silicate, metal-rich ore for the taking. With the Titan project Saturn would be the outer boundary, with the giant Jupiter behind us and Uranus ahead.

But space explorers never, ever ventured outside "the circle." Only probes went out into Wild Space to be monitored by crews safely from their ships or stations within the circle. However, that was for stargazing.

The Navy had the scientists and the Army the soldiers but all space explorers were scientific-minded. Yet, whether they believed in a Creator or not, they both were extremely superstitious about the way of things in outer space. No one talked about it but people did see things—or thought they did.

"It's space sirens," Halley remembered one of the senior drill sergeants, older than dirt, saying to the men in basic around drinks. "They hide just out of our sensors. Watching. Waiting."

Others said it was a form of space dementia characterized by hallucinations. And, of course, others said it had to be extraterrestrials too fearful of us to make contact. We were too primitive or dangerous for their tastes.

Wild Space was where Halley had to go. He felt a knot in his stomach but the intruders were people, not ghosts or aliens. If they were "outside the circle," then it was safe for everyone else, too.

How to get there?

"Sir, I'm not sure what Army is smoking on your ships, but an officer leaving his post is called desertion in the Marine Corps," one of the corporals said to him.

"If you left, it would be desertion. I'm the one who has to go," Halley told him.

"The Copernicus will be here soon though, sir."

"They'll get here and then do everything we've done, wasting a whole lot of time doing it. I can get out there. Be the advance scouting party."

"Party of one, sir. By yourself in Wild Space. Sir, that's crazy. We know how you feel. Your father and all but..."

"Then I shouldn't need to convince you. Forget the sentimentality. We have a missing crew, or we have a confirmed kidnapped crew. Waiting could mean lives."

"You don't know who they are, sir. Or where they are. We're not picking up their transponders."

"They're being jammed. It's the only explanation. You showed me how to see them. Line of sight. That's what we have super-suits for, Marine."

"You can't be serious, sir. You're going to fly 'naked.'"

"Flying naked" was what military called it—using one's own super-suit to fly through space like a ship. In a way, a super-suit was like a wearable spaceship with its own propulsion and air supply. However, the maneuver was completely illegal and permissible only in extreme emergency situations, which this didn't qualify as, stretching alternate interpretations as far as the regs could go.

"Drop me at Ceres in your fancy Barracuda and I'll take it from there," Halley said to them. "Marines, we have almost one hundred crew in danger. I'm the one taking the risk."

"A big risk, sir," said one Marine.

"You get killed out there—" began another.

"Then it'll be the shortest promotion on the books. And I'm OK with that. I'm not OK with sitting here. I'll be your scout. I've done it before for the Marines."

"Yes, you have, sir," another Marine said. "We got the full skinny on you, sir. Wanted to make sure you weren't suffering from some mental disease, running from promotion. Never meet any one of you officers running from that, just always running and looking for the next one. But weren't we surprised to find an Army whose call sign came from us Marines. Why'd they name you Boogeyman, sir?"

"It's classified."

♦ ♦ ♦

Captain Halley got to sit in a new Barracuda-class ship for the first time and Corporal Suess did take him back to Ceres. The Marine stopped and let the captain do a combat exit, then the ship warped away at max burn back to Uroboros. If he was going to be flying "naked," he might as well get used to it.

Soldiers who wanted to be stationed in space had enhanced basic training that those who remained Earthside didn't have to go through. All soldiers, sailors, and Marines went through boot camp to learn basic combat training and marksmanship. Basic training was where one learned to be a soldier and all the history, traditions, and customs. One learned the culture, the mindset, how to work as a team, how to follow orders, and discipline. One learned how to march, dress and groom to military standards, and spit-shine one's boots, as had been done for centuries, and how to make one's bed with the required military corners.

After that, the training got more serious. How to safely handle and maintain one's primary weapon, full hand-to-hand combat training to proficiency, full bayonet and knife training to proficiency, first aid to mastery level, and full bio, chemical, and cyber-terrorism training, including using a protective mask and systems. Then came the battle drills, obstacle courses, grenade qualification courses, land navigation courses, 20K tactical marches, full tactical field training, and endless battle simulation exercises on land, underwater, and in the air.

When the drill sergeants got a hold of you it was their task to transform your civilian brain into a military one. They drilled, worked, ran you until you dropped, and then had you do fifty push-ups for good measure.

But as soldiers being prepared for a career in the "sea of space" in Mil-Sci, it was far more than grunt training. Navy were scientists who had to learn to be soldiers, at least for their time in basic and AIT. Army and Marine soldiering had to include becoming scientific.

Halley remembered the classes well. His platoon wasn't even given the name of the class. All they knew was it was in the giant holographic auditorium. The most advanced virtual reality projectors on Earth and they entered the giant dome dwelling with a perfect star-filled night sky. The instructor entered and asked who in the platoon played baseball. After he saw the hands go up, he asked who thought themselves to be the strongest thrower in the platoon. They all knew Wildman would volunteer. He was cocky about his athletic skills because he was the best compared to everyone else. They'd seen him throw a baseball and everyone swore he could kill a person with his fastball.

"Pick one of the stars and throw your hardest and fastest pitch at it," the instructor told him. "Don't worry. The computer will calculate and project your throw to reach your chosen star, and every star you see is in the Sol system, just like our sun."

Wildman grinned at everyone, took the silver baseball from the instructor, and did his "thing." He went into a steely-eyed trance, waited a few seconds, wound up, and threw the ball so fast, one would think he was throwing his whole arm and not a ball.

The platoon watched the ball go into space at the brightest star. After a few moments, the ball seemed to slowly drift away from the star until it was nowhere close. Wildman tried many more times, then others got their chance. The instructor had his arms folded. The platoon members' eyes had adjusted to the dim light so they could see his inquisitive face.

"What's the problem, grunts?"

Of course, everyone had ideas, but no one was brave enough to be wrong with their guess.

"The stars are in motion, so you need to calculate their trajectory in order to hit them. Wildman, just tell the computer to do so," the instructor said.

"Computer," Wildman began, "calculate the trajectory of the star and what the trajectory of my thrown baseball has to be to hit that star." He smiled at the instructor. How smart he thought he was.

He still missed by a mile.

"If we wait for you all to find the answer for yourselves, we'll be here all century," the instructor said.

"The gravitational pull of..."

"Yes, Halley? Of what?"

"Am I at least close?"

"Very close, warm but not hot. I'll give you the

answer in a language you grunts can understand. Which is more difficult: shooting at a stationary target or shooting at a moving one?"

Everyone answered the latter.

"A moving target and a moving shooter?" he asked. No one knew what to say. "A moving target affected by the gravitational pull of the sun, the planets, asteroids, and a comet that flew by a year ago. A moving target on a moving planet affected by the same gravitational factors. Both in a universe that is moving, swirling, and spinning around."

It wasn't that the stars, Earth, planets, and asteroids were in motion, each with its own gravitational field. Halley never forgot the answer. The entire universe was in motion, too.

Halley had gotten back to his NCS Capricorn on Ceres and then secretly back to the Achilles-2 to get the equipment he needed. He crossed over into Wild Space hours later and exited his shuttle. He walked outside the hull onto the roof.

That class so many years ago with that instructor, now a major on Earth, throwing holographic baseballs at holographic stars showed that even if you could see a target, if you didn't calculate for all variables, you'd never hit a thing. He knew the direction that the cloaked ships had gone but he could look for their distortion field for days, weeks, years, and never see it. In space, being a fraction of a degree off could mean being a million miles off from your target. He needed a solution...now.

Halley fired his bazooka-like device. It flew through space and at a programmed distance, split into a dozen smaller missiles. Miles away, each of the dozen missiles, each split into a dozen more missiles flying deeper into wild space. Halley raised the device again and shot another missile in another grid sector. He kept firing missile after missile, watching the electronic net grow larger and larger on his accompanying battle tablet, which was locked onto the roof of his ship for him to watch.

Hours passed. Halley had fired over four dozen missiles and had over one million sensor data points transmitting back to his tablet for analysis. He was patient as the net continued to grow on its own at a rate of ten percent every thirty minutes.

A red blip on the screen and a second.

Found you!

The first hit he got from his sensor net was from one of the missile probes detecting a non-natural anomaly. The second was from one of the missile probes physically hitting something in space!

Whoever the hostiles were, they had technology that wasn't supposed to exist yet. He wasn't going to take anything for granted and assumed that what the missile detected and bumped off of was a cloaked ship of some kind. More importantly, they knew that they had been located and that he was out there.

Halley climbed back into his ship. In moments, he would be doing his own combat egress.

The explosion lit up space like a mini-star, bright enough to be seen from Uroboros, the Belt colonies, and telescope spotters back on Earth. In seconds, the stargazing community would be abuzz about the photonic burst not far outside the MAB. What none of them would have seen was what Halley did see: the shadow of a ship trying hard to get out of range of the illumination.

Chapter Fourteen

Beacon

The non-military cosmoship Auxiliary Three moved through space under the cover its cloak tech, faster than it ever had since its crew came aboard. The blast of the nearby photo-flare created the desired reaction: They were running. Against its bright light, the distortion field of their cloak made their ship appear to be a great ghostly image in space, formless but not quite invisible to the human eye. They remained invisible to sensors but the low tech of a mini-probe crashing into their hull was a threat. The blinding light finally diminished but they had more of the tiny probes to evade. A cosmoship financed by the best private money could buy, a thousand feet in diameter, running scared from probes the size of a human hand.

The ship's unique design was different from that of any of the military's Nautilus, Argonaut, Blue Whale, or

Whale Shark-class ships. Gravity ring and ship were integrated into one—a spherical ship with a spinning ring.

Inside, the ship was three times taller than most large spacefaring ships but a third in length. The command deck was at the top, the engine deck was at the bottom, and docking at the center opened and closed for small craft to enter.

Two guards in off-white military-style uniforms and matching headgear stood at the end of the long corridor opposite the docking bay doors. The deck had a T-design with the main corridor ending in the ship's three-floor open docking bay. A smaller perpendicular corridor led to the other levels via the lift or steps. Neither guard had the bearing of a military soldier. One even had a few tattoos on his neck and hands. Both had holstered sidearms on their waists.

Lights lining the top of every corridor flashed bright red. Despite Red Alert status, the two guards casually stood at their post without a care. Seasoned sentries came up with their own unique ways to keep sharp and ready despite the boredom, even with blaring sirens in their ears. One whistled a tune to himself. The other passed the time by biting his fingernails.

The sirens finally stopped but the red lights flashed on.

"Why are we out here? Chatter says we're going sideways not forward," a guard said, biting his nails. "Why are we going away from our destination rather than to it? That's why we're getting paid. Sightseeing in empty space isn't my idea of fun."

"We're getting paid. That's all that matters. What would you be doing on Earth if you weren't here? Nothing."

"Oh, it wouldn't be nothing. That much I could swear to."

"But would you be getting paid for it? Chatter doesn't know a thing because they don't tell us a thing. What will you do when you run out?"

"What?"

"When you run out of fingers, what will you chew on then? Are you, like, two years old?"

"Do you hear something?" The guard biting his nails had stopped, listening. They both did.

"What is that? What's that sound?"

They strained their ears as they kept their eyes on the

landing bay doors at the other end of the corridor.

"Should we check it out?"

"No, we stay here. Is that sound getting louder?"

"What is it? It's more like I can feel the sound rather than hear it."

"Yeah, that's it. But what is it? Where is it coming from?"

Clang!

Their eyes locked across the other end of the ten-foot corridor on the sealed bay door.

"Did you hear that?" one asked the other. "No one is supposed to be down there."

"No one is. This ship is a fortress."

"What was that sound, then?"

"Something hit the hull outside, that's all."

"But that was metal."

"Some of those meteorites are like metal when they hit."

Both of them got very quiet, straining their ears again.

"What is that?"

From within the docking bay, the low moan got louder, then stopped. The guards looked at each other.

"Should we call it in? We have to call it in."

"Call what in? You know what the bridge will say."

"I'm not going down there."

"How will we investigate it, then?"

"Then you go. I'll stay here."

"No, we both go."

"We both stay here." The guard began to wince as if in pain. "The sound. You can't hear it but you feel it. It's stronger." The man started to scratch his face, then rubbed his ears.

"We can lie and say we checked it out but couldn't see anything and we need backup."

"Yeah, let's do that. Have them send a team."

Moans. Then the clear sounds of someone choking and gurgling.

"Help me. Help me. I'm lost," the ghostly voice cut the air. "I'm very upset with living people. I want to blow up this deck and suck all the living people into space where I can feed on their bodies."

Both guards ran away as fast as they could down the smaller corridor to the lifts.

◆ ◆ ◆

The ship's Control Room was laid out like a typical military bridge. The conn was in the center with Helm and Tactical on one side, and Sensors and Watch stations on the other. However, the bridge had an additional Engine station. Each station was manned by a single individual on his feet. All the men were dressed in casual military gray fatigues, black tops, black combat boots, and open black cargo jackets.

"Commander, I'm getting a panicked call from guards on the docking deck," a bridge officer called out.

"Handle it!" the commanding officer yelled. "Tactical analysis on the explosion?" he shouted at another.

"Not an explosion, sir. Light only. Some kind of flare gun. No danger," said the Tactical officer.

"Why would someone have an Earth flare gun out here in space? Continue to back us away but slowly. Whoever is out there probably knows exactly where we are despite the cloak."

"Yes, sir," the Helm responded.

"We should fire on them, sir," said Tactical.

"No, their sensor net got lucky. We can back away. Their sensor probes are following a predictable algorithmic progression that we can easily avoid."

"Oh my god. Sir!" yelled the Watch officer.

The commander ran to the man's station to view his display screen. Fog was slowly moving across the floor of the deck.

"Docking deck?"

"Yes, sir."

"Where is it coming from? What were you trying to tell me before?"

"The guards said they heard someone speaking to them from the docking bay."

"What? Why didn't you say that?"

The commander ran back to the conn and hit "red alert."

"Sir, we're already on Red Alert."

The C.O. grabbed the phone from the desk at conn. "Assault teams to docking deck immediately. Possible intruder!" He placed the receiver back on the station. "Reactivate the audible sirens."

"Sir, what's that?" The bridge crewman pointed at the display.

The commander returned to Helm. On his screen, they noticed bright illumination coming from the starboard side of the ship on one of the external surveillance display screens.

"What's that light from? We're cloaked. Find that light...now!"

"Launching Bot One, sir."

"Sir, the entire docking deck is covered by the fog," the Watch officer called out from his station.

"How high?"

"Can't see anything now, sir. The fog is almost to the ceiling."

"Sir!"

Most of the bridge officers pointed to the bridge's main view screen. The commander's eye barely caught sight of what looked like a body quickly floating—but not in a spacesuit. The men looked at each other in shock.

Boom!

The bridge crew jumped.

"Where...explosions," the commander babbled. He ran to the station and grabbed his phone. "Extra security to the bridge, now! Now!" He slammed down the phone. "Oh no! They blew up our gravity ring."

The men began to float as the ship lost all gravity.

The Control Room's main door opened and a three-man security team, along with two frightened guards tried to pull their weightless bodies inside.

Super-suited Halley flew through the open door, grabbed all five men, and threw them back into the corridor. The bridge crew screamed as he flew into Command, grabbed each of the six men, including their captain, arced around, and tossed them into the corridor, too. He punched the button to close the doors.

He stared at them through the door's bay windows as they watched him, so completely overwhelmed and scared out of their minds. Red lights flashing. Sirens blaring.

◆ ◆ ◆

Halley sat at the conn. In only a few days he had sat in the chair of a different ship's commanding officer but not his own ship. The Kauboi and now an unidentified hostile. He wondered what private multinational had built it. What country? The crew aboard the ship hadn't taken the Uroboros crew. They weren't even military. They were civilians, ones who had no business being in space playing pretend soldier. What were they doing flying an advanced cloaked ship? The Uroboros had no crew. This ship had the wrong crew.

Halley stood from the chair. The corridor was empty but he knew none of them had floated far. He punched the button and his back thruster blasted him out as soon as they opened.

As he suspected, the men couldn't even manage to properly float away fast enough to get to a secure part of the ship. They were pathetic wingless angels wearing headgear. Halley flew over them, grabbed the commander by the foot, swung around, and headed back to the Control Room.

A blade popped out of Halley's right arm gauntlet. He cut off the man's right boot, ripped off his sock, and threw them away into the zero-gravity air. The commander's eyes were as wide as baseballs as he pulled back his naked foot in terror. He frantically tried to back away while floating in the air.

"What are you going to do? Leave me alone! I didn't do anything to you," he said in a panic. He tried to swim away through the air.

"Where are they?" Halley asked.

The man stared at him.

"Don't make me ask again. Where's the real crew, and where are your hostages?"

"Hostages? What hostages?"

"The crew of Uroboros Station. Where are they?"

"I don't know. I swear. None of us do. We were hired to fly this ship only. We're not here for any of the military or combat stuff."

"Military or combat stuff, huh?" Halley grabbed the man's naked foot.

"No! I'll tell you what I know!"

Halley turned his head, noticing the movement of glowing shapes at the Sensor station. He slowly flew toward it. The grid showed a part deeper in Wild Space and the glowing shapes moved as a convoy.

"What am I looking at here?"

The man swallowed hard. Halley lifted his bladed arm. "There are other ships in the vicinity. Who are they?"

"I don't know. My orders are to rendezvous with them."

"What nation do they belong to?"

"I don't know. They pay us. We don't ask questions. We fly the spaceships when they tell us."

"Tell me about them."

"They're soldiers."

"What branch?"

"I don't know. They're mercenaries. That's all I know. I swear."

"Before you answer, listen fully to the question I'm about to ask you. If I were to throw your men into space, what would you do to track their transponders?"

The man's mouth hung open in shock. "We haven't done anything to you."

"What would you do? Show me."

The color drained from his face. He pointed to the conn station. Halley grabbed him and pushed his weightless body to it, then watched him closely. The commander typed on the side panel.

"Move aside," Halley said. He had seen enough to know how to work the tracker.

Anyone who worked and lived in space had to agree to mandatory transponder implantation. It was one of the rare times when people, regardless of their politics or worldview, didn't disagree with a government or corporation implanting a piece of tech within their body that transmitted their location from many miles away. The transponder could be jammed in a fashion but it never stopped transmitting unless it was surgically removed. Its real function was in a disaster, if someone was ejected from their ship or station. Besides a random sensor sweep, the transponder was the only way you could be found.

The unique transponder IDs were classified except in the event of an emergency. Before Halley left the Tyson, he'd received a secure transmission with not only the transponder code for his father but also those for the entire Uroboros crew. Halley hoped beyond all odds that the kidnapped crew were still alive. Regardless, what he had to do was find their transponder signals. However, those signals transmitted whether or not the person was alive.

He already had the transponder codes on a screen on his interior display. He began typing, starting with his father's.

Points of light appeared on one of the largest cloaked ships ahead in Wild Space. Halley pointed to the ship on the station screen. "Hostages."

"I don't know anything."

"You work for people, but you don't know anything about them. Go out into deep space with strangers. You expect me to believe that. You and your crew are going to fly me to that ship."

The commander shook his head. "No, we can't. They'll know something's wrong. They probably already do."

"Why is that?"

"We're supposed to check in at regular intervals. They're probably on their way."

"Good. They can take me where I need to go."

"They'll open fire on us."

"With my suit, I can breathe in the vacuum of space for a very long time. Can you?"

The man's face went white as he pointed.

The scene reminded Halley of when the USS Marines had pulled alongside the Uroboros before they boarded. But the ship that pulled alongside was not the Marines. It wasn't visible on the visual display screen but it did appear on the command station as a mean glowing shape twice as long as their ship.

There was a crash and the entire ship rocked.

"It's them! They've docked!" the commander yelled.

Chapter Fifteen

USS Marines

Halley never removed his helmet the entire time he came aboard. The trembling commanding officer probably wondered if there was even a real human within the super-suit or just a cold, killing robot.

From the bridge, Halley watched the landing bay cameras as the doors of the newly docked ship opened. Out flew the copper-suited mercenaries. So, the adults had returned. Halley wasn't quite sure why they left or even needed a group of civilians to fly their cloaked ship but answers "always came to the patient," as one of his instructors in AIT had told him.

One shot. That's all it took and the camera showing the landing bay was gone.

Halley looked at the frightened C.O. floating next to him, then at the entire bridge room.

"They're watching us, aren't they?"

"Yes," the C.O. said nervously.

Halley focused on the display of the bay doors, the entire corridor filled with fog. The door opened, then immediately closed. Halley smiled to himself. The hostiles didn't know what to make of it and had retreated to the docking bay but that wouldn't last long before they acted.

The door opened again and they heard a barrage of gunshots.

"They'll puncture the hull," the C.O. yelled.

"No, the rounds aren't that powerful."

The shots stopped. The docking bay doors opened, then closed.

"What's happening?" Halley asked.

The external cameras showed nothing, as both ships were cloaked. Then Halley saw it. A blip appeared on Sensors, then a Barracuda-class shuttle slammed to a stop alongside. They couldn't see the departing ship but they saw its rail guns at work, showering the hull of the Barracuda with heavy rounds—a giant machine gun in space.

"Big mistake," Halley said.

"Who are they?"

"Marines."

They saw a bright glow from within the Marine's shuttle, then a blinding flash. The explosion caught both Halley and the C.O. off-guard. One second there was nothing, the next the debris of the hostile's cloaked ship was everywhere like a mini-asteroid field of metal had spontaneously come into existence. Pieces from the hostile's ship impacted the Auxiliary Three like a sudden hail storm in space.

"Great. No hostiles to interrogate after all," Halley said, upset.

The Marines' shuttle didn't just carry the best weaponry the military had to offer. It was a weapon—a flying energy cannon.

"I'm taking one of your cloaked shuttles. Make that happen, now," Halley said to the C.O. as he held up his bladed right arm.

♦ ♦ ♦

The Marines boarded and had their entire Auxiliary

Three secured by the time Major Tycho arrived in a second Barracuda with another squad. The ship's entire crew was held in the landing bay with all seventy men holding onto the floor as they floated. What they wanted was to float away, back to Earth to safety. Two Marines guarded them, effortlessly standing in the air with their suits' nozzles automatically blowing air to keep them fixed above the men.

The two Marines had already taken control of the bridge. The remaining six Marines of the first squad strategically stood guard from the landing bay corridor to the command deck. Major Tycho personally interrogated the ship's commanding officer.

"Where's that soldier?" the Major asked the C.O.

"He took one of the small ships."

Major Canaveral motioned to his squad. The Marines left the landing bay for the main corridor.

"Wait!" the C.O. said.

The major turned. "What?"

"That soldier told me to tell you that this ship has external surveillance."

"By whom?"

"The people we work for."

Major touched his shoulder comm. "Rattler. Tasmanian. Stop what you're doing. That bridge has a party line. Make it go away so we can seize this ship. We don't know how many of these hostiles are out there."

◆ ◆ ◆

The two Marines in the ship's Control Room were at the conn and engine stations trying to access all system files.

"On it, major," one Marine said into his comm.

The other Marine had already shifted his focus and begun tapping on his virtual keyboard. He could see the keys in his right ocular piece, fitted like a monocle.

"Found it," he said to his fellow Marine on the bridge.

"Good."

"We got a countdown here."

"Countdown?"

"Eight-three, counting down."

The Marine tapped his comm. "Major, Rattlesnake

has a countdown."

"Countdown? What countdown? What is it at?" Major Canaveral's voice echoed over his comm.

"Sixty-eight, sir."

"Marine, listen to me carefully. Get out of that command room now and I mean not back this way but through. Understand?"

"Copy that, sir."

The two Marines put their helmets back on. One lifted his arm and a rifle popped out. He fired once and the round embedded itself into the ceiling. The contained explosion blew a ten-foot hole into the top of the ship, violently sucking out all the atmosphere as the two suited Marines flew out the breach.

Marines had packed the members of the hostile crew into the small ships, executing dangerous cold launches out of the bay with external docking doors still opening. The major and the other Marines had blown out a section of the hull with explosives too, and were jetting away from the cloaked ship. The two Barracudas had their bay doors open for their Marines to fly in. All were inside.

The cloaked ship exploded. In space, there was no sound. There was a bright orange and yellow flash within the ship as it disintegrated. The explosive cloud disappeared as fast as it appeared but left behind the dust of a ship that once was.

The major cursed in everyone's comms. "I wanted that cloaked ship."

♦ ♦ ♦

The unprofessionalism of the civilians offended Halley. There were no special security measures on their cloaked shuttles whatsoever. Anyone could board and fly off at will. It was unbelievable even to a military newbie who was accustomed to serious security to prevent unauthorized entry to the toilet.

Despite that, the shuttle was smaller than the Dolphin-class but seemed more maneuverable based on his initial run of the ship. The aerodynamic design meant that it was meant for atmosphere and ocean flying as well.

There was a sudden crackling, like static, over his communications.

"Captain Halley, where are you going?"

Halley ignored the transmission. On his sensors display, he could see the nearing convoy ahead, at a dead stop.

"Captain Halley, I'm going to need you to answer. That is a direct order, Army."

"What do you want, Marine?" Halley responded, not recognizing the voice.

"That's Major Canaveral to you, captain."

"Two Marine majors in the same day. What do you want, sir? But I must warn you to save your breath because I'm within spitting distance of my father's location and I'm not in a talkative mood."

"No, captain, I had no intention of talking you out of anything. Can you tell me what you did to this crew over here?"

"Sir? I did nothing to them."

"The corridor to their landing bay was filled with fog. What's that about?"

"Yes, sir, I saw that too when I boarded. The civvies don't seem to know how to make a proper ship. Leaking fog. New one to me too, sir."

"Why is their C.O. missing his boot and sock?"

"Was he, sir?"

"My men tell me you have an interesting call sign, given to you by my colleagues."

"Wouldn't know, sir."

"I got a crew of grown men crying or on the verge of crying because of their encounter with you."

"Sir, may I say that is one fine weapon you Marines have. Is that a real laser cannon, sir?"

"Captain, we're talking about you, not any Marine toys we may or may not have."

"Well, sir, Army may have turned their crew into a group of man-children, but I think it was Marines who blew their parents into atomic particles. I'm going to be losing you soon, sir."

"I didn't call you to chat, captain. Why do you think the hostiles are in Wild Space?"

"I have no idea, sir, and, frankly, I don't give a damn. I'm going to find my father and the rest of the Uroboros crew and if the hostiles give me any problems, I'll be doing a lot more than making them cry and scream."

"Captain, the NCS Nicolaus Copernicus is out there, too. We believe that's why they altered their course."

Halley looked at his screen as the convoy of ships suddenly blasted away at maximum burn. He cursed the air.

Chapter Sixteen

The Nicolaus Copernicus

Halley shot out the cloaked small ship as fast as his back thruster could fire. If the ship convoy sped away from him, then they knew he was there. If they knew he was there, then it was likely a trap and he expected the shuttle to be fired upon. But it was worse.

The self-destruct explosion of the ship threw him spinning into the void of space without control. Luckily, he had been far enough away to not be turned into space dust. However, he hadn't been far enough away to leave his suit systems unaffected.

He slowed his heavy breathing and prayed that he didn't crash into a stray asteroid. His systems came back on and he slowly activated his back thrusters to first slow and stop his spinning, then slow his movement to a dead stop. To float in the vastness of space was both awe-inspiring and terrifying.

Static again on his comms. "May...help..." Little could be done to boost the signal. He had to wait. "This is the NCS Nicolaus Copernicus. Mayday, mayday. We need immediate help. We are under attack by unknown forces."

The first thought that popped into his head was: 'Where was their Marine or Army defense?'

He had a fix on the distress transmission. At full burn, he'd be visible in space like a tiny streaking comet. But that couldn't be helped. There was no way he could catch up to the hostiles in their cloaked ships. But they were flying in the opposite direction.

Who was attacking the Copernicus?

◆ ◆ ◆

A theologian who'd done a civilian spacewalk—finally checking off the item from his bucket list at the age of sixty—said never did he feel more at one with the Deity than when he drifted in the dark void. The sheer terror that, above all things, humans were both objectively insignificant in its wake and ultimately more important than anything else to its Creator. But many of the ponderings from the non-religious were often as profound to the person staring at the infinite magnitude of the universe.

One never tried to understand the universe. One would need a brain the size of Jupiter, so large as to fit one thousand Earths inside, to even begin comprehending it. No, for us with our ant brains, we never try to arrive at an answer. Our quest is to discover the question to ask. Our wisdom, and our path, begin there.

This was what Halley thought about as he rocketed through the dark sea of space. Many studies had been on those who chose military service as their career. Researchers found it remarkable that such a higher percentage of them were religious, despite their being more scientifically astute than the average civilian. It wasn't uncommon for those who went into the Navy to have mastered advanced calculus by middle school. Those in the Army didn't score too far behind, and despite the jokes and perception, the average Marine was far more scientifically minded and mathematically astute than the average civilian too. But then the joke for them became: They only learned math so that they could better blow things up—which was likely true. One said that even those who were clearly atheist or agnostic engaged in practices that could only be described as overtly religious.

But was it religion or superstition? Those in the military services were far more superstitious than any demographic on Earth. Every ship had a chaplain and Navy, soldiers, and Marines wouldn't hear of eliminating the core complement, even if the entire crew were atheists. In a rare flash of cleverness, military Command made it standard for a ship to always have a chaplain, as long as they had double majored and mastered one of the mind services like psychotherapy.

Halley thought, 'If you stare at the universe long enough, can you see it staring back at you?' He was literally flying in space not by sight but by sensors.

Halley closed his eyes and opened them. His mind had gone to religion musings to keep it from going elsewhere. But it was too late. Open space was also scary. The imagination of any adult could be as overactive and ridiculous as any child. He grew up on the same space alien movies as any Earth kid.

"Why?"

Halley asked the question out loud. His ears were sealed by his helmet so his words were fed back to him in real-time through his audio.

Why was the Copernicus here? The Titan mission had been in the works for half a century. Everything had been painstakingly planned every step of the way, every detail, every contingency accounted for. The NCS Nicolaus Copernicus was to arrive one year after the Tyson had made landfall and prepped the designated site for their arrival to begin construction of Earth II. Then he and Captain Ayla were told they would arrive six months early. If the Copernicus was here, they were actually about three months behind the Tyson.

What was going on?

The Uroboros incident. The Kauboi incident. Homesteaders. The Federation. Cloaked ships. Halley had never believed in coincidences when he was a civilian, nor at any time during his fifteen years as a soldier. What was going on?

The NCS Nicolaus Copernicus wasn't just a cosmoship. It was a Blue-whale-class large cruiser twice the size of the Tyson. The significance of the ship was that it transported Earth Alliance's "genesis architects." Planet Tamers MN probably came up with the name for maximum marketing effect among the political and military brass. One would say that until you received the classified briefing of Operation Fairy Dancer and saw their machines in action, as he and Captain

Ayala had, you hadn't seen anything in existence worthy of the term "god-like." After that briefing, one didn't think the name "genesis architect" was stunning enough and one started writing "genesis" in all subsequent communications with a capital "G."

Such a ship would have the best of the best in terms of a Marine complement, with their entire arsenal of deadly toys to protect and defend. Yet they had transmitted a distress signal.

Halley felt the cosmos was testing his resolve, putting one detour and distraction after another in front of him to keep him from getting to his father. But nothing would stop him.

◆ ◆ ◆

Halley saw one yellow flash in the distance but it was no star exploding. He had found the Copernicus.

Fifteen years in the Army and he'd been in a real gun battle only once—the incident that had given him his call sign. Never had he seen an explosion in space, had a ship he served on fire its weapons, had he done a combat spacewalk of any kind, had he flown his super-suit untethered in open space. No one in the military was supposed to have done these things, except Marines, but that had to do with the space mining trade. Ahead was something else a soldier had seen only in simulations and never in real life—a real space battle. Not even the Marines had been in one in space.

Four Barracuda-class shuttle destroyers were all that protected the massive Copernicus hanging in space. Wave after wave of what looked to be one-man fighters or drones in the shape of arrowheads moved faster than any of the Marine craft. The attackers were smart, keeping their attack runs as close to the Copernicus as possible and preventing Marine kill-shots. The ship had energy shields but they would eventually fail against the constant strafing of the attacking ship's rail guns.

Halley was angry inside. Another delay.

Time for a space soldier to earn the day's pay.

"Command, are you reading me?"

"Who...who is this?"

"Command, requesting permission for docking."

"Docking? Who is this? Are you insane? We're under attack."

"Do you have any Marines on board?"

"We're not giving you any information."

"Don't shoot me when I get aboard. Have your C.O. standing by."

"Whoever this is, we'll fire upon any hostile that steps onto our ship."

"I hope that's true because you're not doing a particularly great job shooting those attacking ships. Energy shields don't have infinite power. If you don't blast those attackers out of space or get them to retreat, you'll lose those shields. The Marines can do only so much. We have to do our part. I'll enter through main docking. Have your C.O. standing by."

♦ ♦ ♦

Waiting on the other side of the main docking bay doors were a dozen heavily armed suited soldiers in gray. All their rifles were trained on the door. However, none of the hostiles got a chance to fire. Halley dropped down from a hatch above and beyond them, opening fire and cutting down all the hostiles before his feet landed on the ground. His forearm rifles fell back into his suit as he surveyed the carnage before him. None were alive and he made sure to collect all their loose weapons before he left the deck. If he couldn't secure them, he'd blow them up in a bonfire.

As with any NCS cosmoship, Halley was tracked by surveillance and monitoring cameras and sensors as he flew vertically through the corridors. The command deck was sealed, as he expected, but he could see more than one anxious face peeking through the port windows. He had to follow procedure even if the bridge crew inside knew he was a friendly. Standard protocols were the same for any Mil–Sci ship, whether it was the Copernicus or the Tyson. In the military, there was a standard procedure for everything, including boarding a seized ship.

He set down on the ground and passed his hand over his helmet to go from black visor to clear, so they could see his face. He wouldn't remove his helmet until he was sure he was safe. He stepped to the door so that he could be fully scanned. For a second, he wondered if it was scanning his internal transponder or his dog tags.

"Captain Joshua Halley, USS Army, Commanding Officer of NCS Neil deGrasse Tyson, Military Services."

The door opened. Pointing guns and rifles at him were dozens of men and women in white uniforms and white caps. A woman walked through them to him.

"I see you've finally taken your promotion," she said.

"I have, ma'am."

"Dr. Mayall, Earth Alliance Command, NCS Nicolaus Copernicus."

"Where is your Army contingent, ma'am?"

"Marines only, captain."

"Your entire Marine contingent left the ship?"

"If you come up to the command room, you'll see why they did."

"That will have to wait, ma'am. We have to destroy those attacking ships before you find yourself without energy shields."

"Then the bridge is yours, captain."

◆ ◆ ◆

Halley had his helmet off as he took the conn. The cosmos really was toying with him.

"Tactical, status of our weapons?" he asked.

"Sir, they took all our rail gun turrets," said one of the two officers at the Tactical station.

"Are you telling me we have no functional weapons?"

The officers said nothing. They didn't know what to say.

"Captain, that was what our Marines were for," said Mayall.

Halley marched to Tactical to check the status himself. He typed on the station keyboard, then walked over to the Sensor station, the officer there jumped out of his way. Halley typed on the keyboards.

He launched probe after probe. They could see the attacking manta-ships continue their tight formation strafing of the Copernicus. Halley hit one button. The first probe detonated. The explosive flash immediately destroyed two attacking small ships. A third was damaged, spinning away without power. He hit another button, then another. Two more flashes and this time seven ships were blown apart. The remaining ships retreated at high burn.

"Command, this is Defender Two. That was some kind of improvisation on your part. Using probes as bombs. Brilliant. We didn't think you had it in you."

"Defender Two, we didn't have it in us. We have another visitor to thank," Dr. Mayall said.

"Command, say again. Visitor?"

"Defender Two, yes. I would tell you his call sign, but I don't know it. Other than to say he's Army in one of your upgraded s-suits."

"Command, can he hear me?"

"Defender Two, that's an affirmative," Halley replied.

"Boogeyman, you are to stay put."

Halley pressed the "talk" button. "Defender Two, I'm doing no such thing. I'm sick of all these delays. I told you already, I'm finding my father and the rest of the Uroboros crew and you are to stay the hell out of my way. You are to stop talking to me and take chase after those attacking ships immediately. Make sure they don't get to where they're going. The safety of the Copernicus is your top priority and we don't want to encounter any more hostiles on its trip to Titan. Track and terminate. That's an order!"

"Command, order acknowledged."

They could see the four Barracudas launch away at max burn.

Dr. Mayall and the Copernicus bridge cautiously watched him.

"Note to self, do not make Captain Halley angry," Dr. Mayall said.

Their C and C was identical to the Tyson. Halley had taken off his helmet to review the logs and recordings of the battle. He hadn't seen the larger attacking spaceships where the smaller ones came from. The Marines had left the four Barracudas behind to do the best they could while they took chase in two Orca-class mid-size destroyers. The yellow flash he'd seen was one of the hostile cruisers being blown to bits.

"Their larger ships had energy cannons besides rail guns," the doctor told him. "They managed to damage our Helios with one blast. Destroying those ships took priority. That's why our Marine contingent left the ship."

"Yes, ma'am. You're right but you still seem short on personnel, and I couldn't help but notice that your landing bay is somewhat empty.”

“They are elsewhere but are returning with reinforcements. May I ask a question, captain?”

“Yes, ma’am?”

“How did you get here? We’re grateful, of course, that you were here to deal with our unwelcome guests.”

“I happened to be on an unplanned leave when the Uroboros incident happened, ma’am.”

“Not true, but I won’t push the issue.”

“Ma’am, I need a ship. I’ll borrow the one in your bay.”

“We have only the one in the bay, captain. You can’t take it and leave us without a single craft.”

Halley was visibly upset. “You have escape pods.”

“Captain, you can’t be serious. Besides, you can’t leave until the Marines get back. Whether you like it or not, you’re the senior military officer of the Copernicus. You can’t leave.”

Halley marched back to the conn station and angrily planted his butt in the chair.

“Captain, I can see how emotional you are about this,

but you must help us a bit longer. It's your duty. The mission of the Copernicus and the Tyson is all that matters to Earth Alliance. Our two ships are the Titan mission. Especially after what happened to the KCS Uji Kauboi."

Halley looked up at her. "How do you know about that already?"

"I read your report, captain."

"Already?"

"Yes, captain. Already. The entire crew of a cosmoship spaced. Probably all of Earth Command has read your report. Media probably already has a leaked copy of it, too."

Halley ran his hands through his hair. He was fighting all his impulses to put on his helmet, march to their landing bay, and take their last remaining ship. But the doctor was right. He couldn't. There were only so many lines his superiors would allow him to cross.

"The Copernicus does have the most advanced sensors in the Sol System," the doctor said suggestively to him.

Halley perked up. "Can you see cloaked ships?"

"We may be able to help you there now that we know there are such things as cloaked ships."

"Um, Doctor, sir, um—" one of the bridge officers at Sensors stammered.

"We're in a combat setting so Captain Halley is in charge. What is it?" the doctor asked.

"Sir, another cruiser is headed to us. Different configuration from the ones that attacked us," the junior officer said.

"They're hailing us, sir," said an officer at a station. "It's the Federation."

Chapter Seventeen

The Federation

Halley did the math. Both he and Captain Ayla knew everything about the Copernicus as, separate from the Tyson, it was the most important ship on the Titan Project. The Copernicus had a crew capacity of five hundred—one hundred scientists and techs and four hundred Marines. On this day, they had no Marines aboard and a crew of only fifty.

"Dr. Mayall, where is your crew?"

"Captain, I'm going to have to brief you."

"Doctor, is Operation Fairy Dancer in jeopardy?"

"Jeopardy? No! Not at all. We've accelerated the timetable to prevent any possible jeopardy."

"Doctor, your ship has been attacked. Heavily armed hostiles were aboard your ship in the docking bay."

"We haven't been as successful as we would have liked, but you're here."

"I'm not supposed to be here, Doctor. What is the Federation doing out here?"

"Space doesn't belong to us, captain."

"Don't be cute, Doctor. I've never heard of any Federation ship past Mars. We're going to deny their boarding."

"You can't do that, captain."

"Why not?"

"Because they're responding to our distress calls."

"I responded--" As soon as he said the words, he realized he hadn't. He showed up—out of nowhere. "Are the Earth Alliance and the Federation working together?"

"Captain, I should brief you."

"On what?"

"A lot has changed on Earth as a result of the mission."

"Meaning?"

"Agreements that were finalized and agreed upon by all parties are in flux."

"Doctor, I do speak the English language quite well, as well as a couple of others, but I've never been conversant in political-ese or bullshit. My ship, the Tyson, is going to be on Titan. Your ship the Copernicus, will be joining us to begin terraforming for human colonization. Our two ships are supposed to be the only ones out there for at least a year until a third joins us with the official colonists. Are you telling me that we won't be the only two ships there?"

"I'm saying, captain, that we might not be the only ones going there."

Halley clenched his teeth. He wanted to pound something. "How is that going to work?"

"The Company and the Earth Alliance are working through the situation. What I know is that other nations and other multinationals have reneged on their agreements."

"Are we in some kind of war?" Halley asked.

"I'm not sure, captain. We're trying to avoid a free-for-all in space. But allow the Federation to board and their personnel can help until our people return."

"Help?"

"They have military too, captain. They can keep the ship safe until our people return."

"We're working with the Federation."

"I don't like it any more than you do, captain. I think my animus towards them runs far deeper and longer than yours. But I'm doing this for the sake of the mission. That's all that matters."

Halley turned to the crew at their stations. "Though it seems that you've let most of your crew go off on vacation, do you have any techs on board who can repair the ship's rail guns ASAP?"

"Yes, sir, we can make that happen."

"Then please do so immediately. Also, are you reviewing the logs to make sure such a thing can never be repeated?"

The crew looked at each other. Dr. Mayall nodded reassuringly to them. "Captain, that will also be done immediately. Please have patience with us. We're not military. We're terraformers."

"You're not terraformers yet, Doctor. Technically, there is no such thing. All of it is fantasy until we do it.

Until then, you'll have to be military for all of us to keep this ship and all aboard safe."

"Yes, captain. You're right."

"How long until the Federation gets here?" Halley asked the bridge crew.

"They'll be here in twenty minutes, sir."

"Then let's get all our work done before then."

Federation spaceships all had the same saucer design. Earth Alliance called them flying hub-capped tires. Earth Alliance consisted of the unified nations of the world, but the Federation were the unaffiliated nations that wanted a true world government. Halley knew it was far more complicated than that, but if there was a simplistic comparison, it was the world that ran the lucrative space mining industry and those that didn't. Halley was a soldier but not a naive one. The Federation's growing global membership included politicians, scientists, industrials, intellectuals, entertainers, and lots of young people—with a whole lot of wealth and connections behind them. Earth Alliance Command was afraid of the Federation.

From the bridge, on the main view screen, they could see the Federation saucership getting closer.

"Command, this is the Federation Spaceship Venturer, responding to your distress transmission. Requesting permission for docking."

"Venturer. Permission for docking granted."

Dr. Mayall turned to one of the bridge officers. "You're acting XO. Greet our visitors."

"Yes, ma'am," one of them responded and gestured to a couple of others. The three of them left the bridge.

"Captain, I can take it from here," the doctor said.

"Ma'am, I think that would be best. I might engage in behavior and language unbecoming of an officer."

Halley, Mayall, and the remaining bridge officers watched everything from the time the Federation contingent came aboard. Mayall noticed Halley turning his head to stifle a laugh.

A man in a golden tunic and black pants was surrounded by male and female personnel who looked like Terran police officers with red tops, black pants, and black caps. The Copernicus officers led them to

Command and Control.

As the door opened, Dr. Mayall greeted the Federation officer with a handshake. "Dr. Mayall of the Copernicus."

"Commander Andromeda of the Federation Venturer."

The Federation personnel noticed Halley standing at the conn in his super-suit without his helmet.

"This is Captain Halley, our Army officer on loan, so to speak," Mayall said.

"I believe I've heard of you," Andromeda said. He looked at both the doctor and Halley as he spoke. "We've been monitoring the situation. The Federation can take charge."

"Take charge?" Halley asked. "The Copernicus asked for assistance, not for you to take charge."

"Captain, there are other hostiles are out there," Andromeda said.

"These hostiles that attacked us, who are they? Where did they come from?" Halley asked.

"We call them Wanderers and they could have come from any number of countries. They're unaffiliated even with their own countries.”

“How do these unaffiliated civilians get to deep space?”

“I suppose the same way the rest of us do, captain. They fly a spaceship.”

“Getting help. Maybe from the Federation?”

“The Federation has no connection with these people.”

“Tell me about the Homesteaders.”

Andromeda could never be a poker player. His face clearly telegraphed his internal emotions.

“It won’t work,” Halley said.

“What won’t work?” Andromeda asked.

“Earth Alliance Command will never allow the Federation to send civilians to Titan.”

Mayall was now interested. “Sending civilians to Titan? What is the captain talking about?”

“I know what the ancient meaning of a ‘homesteader’ is,” Halley said to him and then turned to Mayall. “They’re financing civilians to take their spaceships to Titan.”

"What? I never heard of this," Mayall said.

"Because it's not true," Andromeda said.

"Earth Alliance has exclusive claim to Titan," Mayall said.

"How can you have exclusive claim to a moon or planet?" one of the Federation redshirts asked. "They don't belong to anyone."

"How dare you risk these people's lives," Halley yelled at Andromeda. "They could die out here. And you'd better hope we never prove that these attackers were also your doing."

"You have quite a low opinion of us," the same Federation redshirt said. "We were answering your distress call."

"Why are you out here?" Halley asked. "Since when is the Federation in deep space?"

"Space exploration," the redshirt said facetiously.

"Dr. Andromeda, I'm very disappointed in what I'm learning," Mayall said. "This has all been settled on Earth. You're circumventing the very agreements we all reached. If you attempted any colonies on Titan, they would be expressly forbidden."

"You one-worlders can't succeed with your one-world on Earth, so you're trying for a one-solar system government instead," Halley said. "World governments never seem to work out, do they, but there are always people like you who keep trying. We had one championed by a fascist sympathizer and bigot who happened to be a president. Another version couldn't distinguish between good and evil and had mass murderers on their human rights committees. Another was run by shadowy billionaires sneaking around in the darkness hanging out with slave traffickers and dictators to amuse themselves. The Earth Alliance will be no part of your Federation. World government always means the same thing: your life is ruled by elites far, far away, unelected and unaccountable to the people.

"A very interesting name—the Earth Alliance, which, strangely, doesn't include most of the countries on Earth," the redshirt officer said to him. He was, of course, correct.

"It includes the space-faring countries of Earth and it's a voluntary organization. Better than naming ourselves after an organization from some ancient kids show. You do know warp drive and time travel aren't real, right?"

Andromeda had had enough. "I can see we have a lot

of ill will and misconceptions about the Federation and what it is and what it isn't," he said. "We aren't forcing anyone to join us. We're simply an alternative. You accuse us of wanting a monopoly of sorts, but that's exactly what you want for yourselves. Why should you be the sole entity to 'tame planets' for human colonization?"

"Do whatever you want Federation. Just stay out of my way," Halley said.

"Again, we're responding to your distress signal," Andromeda added.

"Tell me about these Homesteaders."

"You met them?"

"Can you tell me why the Federation is encouraging civilians to come out into deep space without a clue as to what they're doing?"

"We're not encouraging people to come out here to die, if that's what you're suggesting. They will be under Federation protection and guidance."

"Yes, new members for your great Federation."

"Mister..."

"I'm not a mister. I'm a captain in the USS Army."

"No disrespect intended, captain."

"Sorry but I'm not in the friendliest mood. I need a ship."

"Bear with me a moment, captain. When was the last time you were on Earth? Properly. Away from the cocoon of Mil-Sci?"

"What are you trying to say?"

"I take that to mean it has been a while. You truly don't know what's been going on."

"Five years, to answer your question."

"Then I'd recommend you get your great Earth Alliance Command to properly brief you on the goings on back on Earth and how what's been going on there will have a very direct impact on Operation Fairy Dancer."

"You know the name. Well, that's classified."

"Then let me speak in an unclassified language: the Titan mission."

"As much as I'd like to continue this conversation, I have some cloaked ships to find, track, and board."

"Cloaked ships?"

"Yes."

"May I propose a plan that might be mutually beneficial?"

"Which is?" Halley asked him.

"Your Earth Alliance isn't here. We are. We'll give you a ship."

"In exchange for what?"

"Consideration."

"You all even talk alike. The Homesteaders helped me and said something very similar."

"Then you can see that to help our fellow human being is in our nature, despite your suspicions and unfairly linking us with a history that has nothing to do with us today. The Federation isn't the United Nations or a kids' show. We're an organization trying to form a world alliance of all its nations, not a government to tell you what to do in your own hometown. We think a unified humanity across the globe is something to be strived for to continue our collective evolution."

"Evolution to what?"

"A better human, captain. To be better in this vast cosmos of ours."

Any outsider watching Halley and Mayall would say it was Earth Alliance that sounded like the barbarians. However, Halley would never trust their altruistic, intellectual, all-peace-and-love talk. He had dealt with them before. But he accepted that the the Federation had won this verbal round. He wasn't so filled with ego that he was beyond putting his tail between his legs and standing down when the situation called for it.

"May I suggest that you take advantage of us being here," Andromeda said. "Again, we are responding to your distress signal. Do you want our assistance or do you want us to leave? This is your ship. Tell us what you want to do."

Dr. Mayall replied, "We would welcome any assistance until our Marines return."

"They went after the hostiles," Halley added.

"Then, captain, another ship to provide defense for the Copernicus?" Andromeda asked.

"Yes, that would be fine," he replied.

"The Venturer has its own shuttle fighters. We can have them take up orbiting positions around your ship for added defense," the main redshirt said.

"Yes, that would be fine."

"How many of these shuttle fighters do you have?" Halley asked.

Mayall threw an unapproving look at him. "Captain, we've had this conversation before."

"Yes, we have. I need a ship."

"We can lend you a ship," Andromeda said casually. "All are equipped with micro-Helios engines."

"Your shuttles are equipped with Helios engines?" Halley asked. Mayall was also incredulous.

"Yes, all our craft do."

Halley looked at Mayall. "I can catch them. No doubt about it now."

Mayall's resolve was collapsing. "Looks like I have no more leverage to keep you here, captain."

"Show me where their cloaked ships are on Sensors and I can get our hostages back."

"Hostages?" Andromeda asked.

"Uroboros Station's crew was taken by these hostiles in cloaked ships," Mayall said. "Your faces tell me that you know who these people are."

"They've attacked us, too," Redshirt said. "They're

criminals. They capture crews and ransom them back to their companies or governments."

"We've never heard of this before," Mayall said.

"Because you never hear about anything outside Earth Alliance. For us, this has been going on for years," Redshirt said.

"They're very dangerous," Andromeda said.

"I'm very dangerous, too," Halley said.

"Then let's get you into a Federation shuttle, shall we?"

Chapter Eighteen

The Sargasso Sea

The Helios engine made deep-space travel possible and undoubtedly would be the foundation for even more powerful engines. In his top-secret capacity, Halley knew this to be true, as he had already piloted the next version. He often wondered if others with even higher security clearance had the next phase sitting in a secret bunker somewhere.

Mil-Sci would never put a Helios engine on any craft smaller than a mid-size cosmoship. They were too powerful—and expensive—to use otherwise. But Halley was using a Helios-powered Federation shuttle to get to his destination. For the time being—and this time only—he was grateful to the Federation for being different from Earth Command.

Military craft were built for modest comfort, not

luxury. However, the Federation shuttle reminded Halley of a limo on Earth rather than a spaceship. The controls were also not military configuration in any way. Any novice off the street could operate it, which no military or multinational would ever sanction. Halley actually got a bit angry as he looked at the labeled buttons. MUSIC? Space was inherently dangerous. It was why all military personnel wore their zero-belts at all times. Despite all the precautions, sensors, energy shields, and mini-projectile defense systems, both machines and systems could fail. Some rock that had begun its flight a thousand years before you were born could puncture your ship's hull and pull the air out of your lungs, or, worse, snatch your body into the void of space. Music? The civilian designers of the super-suit had wanted to add the feature many decades ago. The military branches couldn't shut down the preposterousness of the idea fast enough. R&R was for music, not soldiering time.

The same applied to cosmoships. They weren't supposed to be comfortable, they were supposed to keep you alive. That was all that mattered. Halley shook his head at the other buttons: CLIMATE CONTROL and HEAT. The democratization of space exploration? That was why he hated the Federation. Those who lived and worked in space, like him, knew how truly dangerous it was if one didn't know what one was doing. No one deserved to die in space, and no one should in this century.

But he had a ship for his "mission." He had the intel from the Copernicus and the Federation so he knew where he was going—right back to the MAB, but to a section he had never seen or heard about before.

For most of his career, he'd spent every waking moment preparing for the Titan mission. He had actually met someone in training who'd been on the project for eighty years. Halley was beginning to realize that he'd done so at the exclusion of everything else but so did a lot of people working in deep space. Space explorers didn't leave Earth to then focus on Earth. But how much did they not know of things back on Earth that would directly intrude into deep space and their lives?

When the asteroid mining gold rush began, multinationals had sent out probes for years to find the richest deposits. But with millions of asteroids, he'd always wondered if the decisions were made for convenience. The section of the MAB closest to Mars was where Earth's space mining empire was built. Now he knew there were other sections.

He vaguely remembered hearing the term—the section of the Main Asteroid Belt opposite Mars, colloquially known as the "Sargasso Sea." But unlike the Terran version in Earth's Atlantic Ocean, a vast patch of free-floating seaweed called Sargassum, this part of the MAB was mostly uncharted.

The Sargassum on Earth provided a home to an amazing variety of marine species. He'd now learned that the section of the MAB given the same name provided a home to a new group of mysterious humans. He didn't like it.

◆ ◆ ◆

In the minds of many, the asteroid belt always looked crowded. However, that was only if you were the size of the sun passing through it. The asteroid looked quite empty in a shuttle-sized ship but what Halley saw was the opposite.

Halley dead-stopped his Federation shuttle and stared out the main bay observation window. Something wasn't right. Why would one part of the MAB be almost empty when the section before him was so thick with asteroids that even a tiny shuttle would have trouble maneuvering through it? In space, getting hit by anything was a big deal. Any potential breach of the hull meant compromised life support, which could kill people. Real space explorers acted like their ships were made of tissue paper.

Simulated. That was what Halley surmised as he watched the asteroids. The asteroids were man-made. It was the only logical explanation. Were they created to conceal? Were they some type of automatic defense system? Could they move on their own like bots, or the asteroid ship he secretly piloted to get to the MAB? How could someone construct a field of fake asteroids without anyone in Earth Command knowing?

The shape streaked past the front of his ship. Halley acted instinctively and raised the blast shields over the main bay window, switching to view screen mode. Down he flew as the sensors showed him that whatever had passed his ship was arcing back around to him.

He hesitated, then pushed the STEALTH button on the main console. The shape on the sensors stopped. The attack bot was searching for him but apparently its sensors couldn't detect him anymore.

"These cartoon controls actually work," Halley said to himself.

Halley didn't wait, in case the bot tried to calculate

his location based on the previous heading. He maneuvered in a completely different trajectory. The attack bot moved slower but still in the direction it thought his shuttle would be. With power off, Halley let the shuttle drift away on its own inertia. Two more sentry bots arrived, flying fast through space as Halley's ship floated into the asteroid field.

The rocks in the fake asteroid belt ranged from the size of a large cosmoship in length and width down to the size of his shuttle, then to the size of baseballs and pebbles. These tiny rocks worried Halley. Were they real or fake? If fake, what was their purpose? Fortunately, they bounced off without sticking to the hull.

In flight school, they had gone through many "asteroid belt" simulations. Never had he expected to have to use those skills in real life. For the average soldier, space travel involved flying in a straight line into blackness one way, then back the same way to return. Halley found himself turning sharp left or right, rising or dipping, accelerating and decelerating fast to avoid the bigger rocks. His erratic flying to stay in one piece seemed to go on for hours. He was flying by sensors alone, quickly responding to a myriad of data to avoid even a scratch on the ship. He didn't want the Federation to say that a soldier from Earth Alliance had damaged their property.

As he emerged, he saw it. At first, he thought he was seeing things. Another asteroid orbital station very much like the Uroboros Station hung in the distance off a huge asteroid twice its size.

He saw a single flash from the station. Every light within his shuttle flashed red, with sirens blaring.

"Incoming object! Incoming object!" the computer voice repeated.

The commander sat at his station, intently watching the view screen. He was a big man wearing the same black augmented uniform as his bridge crew—covering every part of the body up to the neck, not as bulky as a regular space suit but thicker. He hadn't shaved in weeks. Black hair, spotted with gray, covered half his face from under his nose and extended down to a beard with a rubber band around the tip. His teeth were all metal. Their removal was a common practice among mercenaries. His hairstyle was a buzz-cut. Other members of the bridge crew either were bald or had tied their long hair in a bun or hard-braided it down their back.

Whoever was piloting the intruding ship managed to hop it before the full force of their round struck it. The bridge crew watched pieces of the ship float apart.

"Whatever genius invents long-range life-reading sensors will instantly become one of the richest people on the planet," the commander said, more to himself than the crew.

The interior of the ship was covered with metal reinforced plating. The interior of their spacious command was the same, but unlike the circular layout of most bridges, with command in the center, all stations were against the wall. The conn was in the center with a full console table in front of him, so he could see both the large view screen on the wall ahead of him and the sensor display below eye level. The bridge had over a dozen different stations, with a man at each post.

"Do we have that ship in the registry?" he asked.

"No, sir. But it must be a Federation ship," an officer said.

"So, Earth Alliance and the Federation are out here."

As the pieces of the ship drifted toward their station, the captain stood from his chair. "Why are those ship fragments approaching us? Shouldn't they be moving away from us into the asteroid belt?"

"Yes, commander."

He looked at his crew. "The pilot is alive."

"Military, you think?"

"Whatever. Let's greet them accordingly," the commander said with a grin as he sat back down. "Comm, send a hail."

"Sir? Hail who?"

"Open all channels."

"Channels open, sir."

"Hello, intruder. We can see you," he said playfully. "Do you plan to visit us without so much as a 'hello'?"

"Where's the crew of the Uroboros?" Halley's voice came over the comms.

"I'm very disappointed in you. You should have stayed quiet. Played along longer."

"Where's the Uroboros crew? I won't ask again."

"Why do you want to know? Maybe they're visiting."

"Is this funny to you? My father is part of that crew, so I apologize if I don't join in the fun and games. But

I'll be up to the bridge shortly to give you an attitude adjustment."

The captain stood up from his chair again. "I'll put the kettle on for some coffee." He made a neck-cutting gesture to the crew.

"He can't hear us, sir."

"Put the station on high alert until we kill this bastard."

But before the bridge crew member could activate, the station's alert sirens and lights erupted. Something had happened.

◆ ◆ ◆

The three main pieces of the Federation shuttle hit the orbital station just as an explosive device blew apart its gravity ring. A simultaneous explosion destroyed the entire sensor and comms array on top of the station.

"Sir, all sensors are gone! Comms too!"

"All hands, we're under attack!" the commander yelled into the overhead comms. "Prepare for hostile boarding!" He floated to the bridge's secure weapons vault in a corner of the floor. Then he placed his palm on the plating. "Zed Zed Beta One Three Niner." The plating cover opened and he pulled out weapon after weapon, throwing collapsible rifles to his floating crew. "Half of you, secure this deck from both ends! The other half, get to the armory and get what we need. They have to be Earth Alliance military."

"But it was a Federation shuttle, sir."

"This is no Federation! Move!"

"What about you, sir?" a crew member asked.

"Forget me! Kill this bastard."

"Do you think it's just one?" another asked.

"No. You saw the size of their ship. I'd say there are seven to a dozen of them. They'll try to board the station from multiple points, probably all at once. They wear those advanced tech super-suits, so we need our weapons. Move!"

The lights went off but emergency lights quickly came on.

"Move!" the commander yelled again.

The entire bridge crew floated out the main door. The commander immediately locked it behind them and then activated the emergency barrier—another layer of thick doors to prevent entrance.

"You won't be getting in here, bastards!"

He turned and found the muzzle of a gauntlet gun pointed between his eyes. A seven-foot soldier in a super suit hung in zero gravity like a terrible avenging angel.

"I did tell you I'd be up soon for your attitude adjustment," Halley said.

The captain swallowed hard.

◆ ◆ ◆

The captain mentally kicked himself as the super-soldier used handcuffs to fasten his hands, then his legs, to the conn chair. Though the handcuffs were made of plastic, it was the kind of plastic that was as strong as steel. He wouldn't be breaking out of them even with all the strength he could muster.

"Who are you?" Halley asked.

"Captain Hermes."

"Captain Hermes is your name. Kidnapping crews is your game, is it?"

"I was following orders."

"Where is the Uroboros crew?"

"What happens if I don't tell you? Torture has been illegal in the Earth Alliance for centuries."

"I see my attitude adjustment needs a bit of fine-tuning. You want games? Here are some games for you to play."

A blade popped out of his gauntlet. With two quick slashes, Hermes' hands were free, then two more and his feet were free. Halley grabbed Hermes by the belt like a rag doll, then flew to the escape pods. A look of sheer terror came over Captain Hermes' face when he realized what Halley was doing. He launched an empty escape pod, waited, then blasted open the door. Halley pried open the latch and slammed Hermes' body into the empty capsule launcher.

Hermes raised his hands, his whole body trembling.

"Put me back in the chair and I'll answer anything you want to know! My attitude is better. It's better!"

"Any more games?"

"No."

"If I don't find the Uroboros crew and my father in

quick fashion, I'll blow apart this entire station and I won't lose one second's sleep after watching you float away toward the planet UR-ANUS."

"I'll answer anything you want to know. Put me back in the chair."

The power of a military super-suit was something to fear. Halley threw Hermes at the chair with such force, he almost knocked the man unconscious when his body crashed into it, even in zero-gravity. In less than a minute Hermes was tied to the chair again, both hands and feet.

"What is a Captain Hermes?"

"I run this station."

"For who?"

"Umbra."

Halley's face wasn't visible to the man. All Hermes could see was a black faceplate staring back at him.

"You know Umbra?" Hermes asked.

"How long has this station been here?"

"I've been here two years. I don't know how long it was here before that."

"Its mission?"

"Space mining."

"That's all?"

"Surveillance and spaceport for Umbra ships."

"And?"

"That's all. Nothing else. Private space mining is what we do, away from everyone else."

"What about the Uroboros crew?"

"They took the crew from Uroboros as a diversion, I guess."

"Diversion for what?"

"Delay them—you, your people. For our convoy to make its flight."

"To where?"

"Titan, of course."

"What about the Earth Alliance? They were on their way first."

"One Nautilus-class cruiser is no match for our convoy."

Halley popped Hermes in the nose.

"What was that for?"

Halley ignored him. "Where's the crew?"

"They're on the Randy Roger."

"What's a Randy Roger?"

"It's our elite attack cruiser. Their crew is real ex-military."

"Good. I'm real military, so it'll be a fair fight."

"You won't be able to do to them what you did to us."

"We'll see. Maybe after this you'll stay on Earth where you belong."

"You don't have your Federation shuttle anymore. You'll never get to our docking bay, and even if you could, you'll never get one of our ships."

"Why do I need to get to your docking bay? I already have a ship—a very big ship. I even have my own XO who can navigate straight to the Randy Roger to rescue the Uroboros crew and my father. What do you think, my newly appointed XO?"

The criminal commander stared at him in disbelief.

Chapter Nineteen

The Randy Roger

Halley sat in another captain's chair, staring through his dark visor at the main observation bay window ahead and the sensor display table, which he had Hermes collapse into the floor.

"Are you sure you want to do this?" Hermes asked, standing at the navigation station.

"As opposed to what? Waiting here for your fellow mercenaries to break in? I know you sent them to your armory."

Hermes looked up at the ceiling. "How did you get on my station and onto my bridge?"

"When I depart, you can spend as much time as you need to figure it out. ETA to our target?"

"The Bodacious Betty will be at the Randy Roger's

backside in less than two hours at current speed."

"We have people naming their vessels after great scientists, constellations, and other galaxies, but you name yours with juvenile names like a child."

Hermes chuckled. "What happened to the good ol' days when military guys and gals spoke with red-blooded human profanity and debauchery?"

"We'll leave that behavior for you mercenaries."

"I'm not a mercenary."

"Still with the games. Just as civilians can spot us by the way we stand, walk, and talk, we can spot each other. Also, if you wanted to pretend to be a civilian, you might have skipped the metal dental implants."

"No fooling you."

"Were you always a gutter-crawling mercenary and kidnapper? Exactly the kind of person Umbra would hire."

"There it is. That's why you don't appreciate my infectious charm. You're envious of my employer."

"Is that what Umbra is? You work for a criminal corporation."

"Criminal. You live a sheltered life, soldier. What do you think Planet Tamers Multinational is? How do you think they got to where they are now? All you are is an over-paid bodyguard for a corporation pretending to work for the military when you actually work for them."

"Hermes, I've been a soldier for fifteen years. Do you really believe I haven't heard your propaganda from civilian idiots a million times before?"

"I had to try. You wouldn't respect me if I didn't try to do something."

"I'm active service. I know what's real and what's not. Conserve your air and get me to the backside of your Randy Roger."

"What do you suppose will happen when they spot their orbital asteroid station flying through space to them rather than where it's supposed to be?"

"They won't blast us out of space. That's all I care about."

"They're real military, you know."

"You told me already."

"As long as you're prepared for what's coming."

"As long as you know that if I don't get the Uroboros

crew, Roger won't be Randy when I'm done with him."

"And your father. What's his name, by the way? He must be quite a man too if he raised a fine soldier like you."

"His name is Mirosław Hermes."

Hermes erupted in laughter. "He has the same name as me?"

Halley wasn't taking any chances. He assumed that either the Betty's crew or others were watching every move he made on the locked down bridge.

"You're either very good or very paranoid. No one's watching us, soldier. Will you at least tell me your name? I am your appointed XO, after all."

"Landonis Balthazar 'Lando' Calrissian."

Hermes laughed again. "Live long and prosper to you, too."

♦ ♦ ♦

None of it made any sense.

If Umbra was behind the kidnapping of the Uroboros crew, that would be a criminal act. But Umbra MN was by no means a criminal corporation. They were one of Planet Tamers' corporate rivals. Many called themselves "terraforming" companies these days, but the fact was that no conglomerate had terraformed any planet yet. Many multinationals said they could and lobbied governments hard. Ultimately, Planet Tamers had been awarded the Earth Titan contract over all others not because they were the most politically savvy (which they were), treated and paid their employees better than all others (which they did), or had the best technology (which, based on what he'd seen in the last few days, Halley wasn't sure about anymore). Nations and their armed services couldn't care less about that. Who could make the Titan project happen and usher in the next chapter of humanity—becoming a multi-planet species faster, safer, and more cost effectively than anyone else? Planet Tamers got the contract because they had already pioneered the space mining industry and almost single-handedly made the MAB colonies a reality. They had a thirty-year advantage over all other multinationals, including Umbra.

What gave Halley a bit of concern was that for nations not part of the Earth Alliance, the Federation was their Planet Tamers MN. But for those who didn't want to be part of "polite society," there was Umbra.

Halley had heard a sound at the secured main doors to the bridge. It was the second time and he knew that the Betty's crew was up to something.

"Hermes!" Halley yelled.

The man turned from Navigation to look at him.

"Put on your helmet."

Hermes looked unhappy but complied. His helmet rested on one of the stations. It took him a second to put it on. He peered through the faceplate that went from the forehead to the chin, clearly showing his full face. His body language conveyed that he, too, felt that something was going to happen. The man didn't or couldn't say it, but he appreciated that Halley still thought of the welfare of others, even someone he considered an enemy.

"You know, soldier," Hermes said, "out here is the Wild Wild West. No sheriff to patrol the territory. I don't kidnap people and I never have. My bosses did but not us. I don't know why they did it but they don't do things like that without a good reason. Maybe your Uroboros did something to them. Maybe they were in the wrong place at the wrong time. I don't know. Ask them when you get to the Roger."

"I intend to."

"I don't recommend it. You should escape while you can."

"What's our new ETA?"

"Less than an hour, assuming no other asteroid tries to hit us."

"How many of these fake asteroids did you make?"

"I didn't make any of them. We protect the crews that do. The asteroids are our defense net…from people like you."

"We didn't know you were here."

"That's the best defense money can't buy. When your enemy doesn't even know you exist."

"Why am I an enemy? If you hadn't kidnapped the Uroboros crew, I wouldn't even be here and would never have known of you. You brought all this on yourself."

"I hope things work out for you. I doubt they will, but I'll say it just the same."

"You'd better keep your eyes on the road. I don't want us crashing into any asteroids or cloaked ships."

Halley watched for a reaction, but Hermes simply

looked at the displays at his navigation station.

Hermes hadn't noticed it, but Halley was no longing sitting in the chair. Instead, he was floating a couple of inches above the seat via his suit's nozzles. His audios could hear the heartbeats and heavy breathing of those gathering outside the main entrance and its barrier. He could hear even their whispers as if they were yelling. They weren't speaking English or any of the other four international space languages.

But he knew. They were coming in.

◆ ◆ ◆

"They're here," Halley heard one of them whisper from the other side of the doors. "Do it!"

The explosion ripped off the main doors with such speed and force that if anyone had been standing there, they could have been killed instantly. Only fools or the utterly ruthless would have detonated a bomb on a space station of any kind. He knew it was the latter, as he realized what their "they're here" comment meant.

What emerged from the smoke of the bomb was not the black-uniformed mercenary crew but a force in sparkling copper-colored exo-suits. Several rushed in with large rifles pointed.

Hermes had his back on the floor and his arms above his head. The smoke from the explosion billowed across the bridge.

"Where is he?" one of them asked.

"I didn't see where he went," Hermes cried.

"Why did you bring him here?"

"I had no choice."

"Yes, you did." The copper soldier fired multiple times. Hermes lay dead on the floor with his helmet shattered around him.

"Fire into the smoke! We'll find him that way!"

Floating just below the ceiling in his super-suit, Halley didn't wait for them to fire. He didn't know the density of their armor, so the rounds fired from his forearm gauntlets were the most lethal but short of being powerful enough to puncture the station's hull. The soldiers screamed as they were cut down.

Halley dropped to the ground as the station's mercenary crew in the outside corridor fired from large multi-barrel rifles. He tossed another explosive round. The black-uniformed crew tried to run. The stun explosion sent them all flying into the walls and ceilings.

Halley grabbed the soldier who had killed Hermes. He violently stomped the helmet from the soldier's head. The shocked man stared up at him with blood in his mouth.

"You like to kill people, do you?" Halley asked, leaning down over him. "Hermes was my appointed XO to take me to the Randy Roger, so now the job falls to you. Thanks for bringing me one of your cloaked ships to get there. Let's go."

Halley grabbed the soldier's leg and dragged him across the floor, out of the main entrance into the damage and bodies in the corridor to the docking bay.

◆ ◆ ◆

Halley dragged his prisoner all the way to the landing bay, always keeping an eye on him and a finger on his trigger. The stimulant Halley had injected him with would keep the soldier alert for the distance to the Roger, despite his wounds.

"I will do nothing to help you," he snarled. "I'm no traitor and nothing you can do to me will make me help you."

Three of the small ships waited in docking. They were spherical ships with circular bulbs geometrically lining the outside hull. The vessels were the only craft that could be the cloaked ships, as they were unlike any construction he had seen.

"You will never get in," the soldier said, trying not to cough blood again.

But Halley did know. He and the Marines had carefully watched all the secret recordings of the Uroboros and had seen the copper soldiers exit and enter their then-invisible ships. Halley grabbed the hand of the soldier, who was helpless to resist, and placed the gloved palm on the door. It opened and Halley threw the man inside.

The soldier looked like a wet, enraged animal on the floor of the ship ready to explode.

"You'd better relax before you hurt yourself," Halley directed as he stepped in like an automaton.

"You will never get to our ship. We'll blast you out from space."

"You mean 'we.'"

"I'm not afraid to die."

"Yes, I can see that. You have that fanatical stench about you. Another group that has no business in space."

Halley studied the ship. He fired once at the soldier, rendering him unconscious. There was no place to secure him and Halley certainly didn't want him moving around. He sat in one of two pilot seats and scanned the controls. There was no "POWER UP" button like in the Federation shuttle, but the controls were standard international military configuration, which he knew in his sleep. The ship wouldn't "power up."

"Command not recognized," said the computer voice. "Please repeat your command."

"Immediate launch into space."

"Commencing pre-launch systems. Launching vessel in fifteen seconds. Secure all personnel and cargo."

Halley sat back in the chair.

"Launching vessel," the computer said.

"Activate cloak," Halley commanded.

"Engaging primary defensive systems, including visual occlusion shield and sensor jamming."

"Transfer helm to manual controls."

"Auto-pilot disengaging."

The main bay opened to space and he slowly flew forward.

"Computer, are there any other ships in the vicinity?"

"Affirmative. Two nightshade-class ships fore."

Had he not disengaged the auto-pilot, he would have been dead. Both cloaked ships opened fire as he went into defense maneuvers.

◆ ◆ ◆

So many things had happened that Halley had never experienced in his entire military career. Things had been done that one did not do in space. The two ships didn't open up rail fire as he expected. They fired some type of energy plasma rays. The Betty could survive rail-gun fire but not energy ray blasts. The brief explosions consumed the entire docking bay. The space station would follow and everyone aboard would be sucked into space. They were killing their own people to get him.

In Mil-Sci, it took months to become certified in

flying a ship for combat, then more months to master firing its weapons to be able to hit anything other than open space. Flying an unfamiliar ship and firing its weapons was considered madness.

"What offensive weapons do I have available?" Halley yelled.

"Vessels are equipped with alloy-round rail guns, plasma energy turrets, and four laser-guided guided missiles," the computer replied.

"Fire missile one at first target!"

"Incoming missiles!"

Halley had no idea how powerful the blast would be. They had him trapped within the bay. He had no intention of finding out.

"What's happening?" The soldier had awoken.

"Shut up!"

Halley whipped the ship around in a complete one-hundred-degree turn. The soldier's handcuffed body crashed against the side of the ship. He'd have to fly through the ship.

♦ ♦ ♦

Halley's spherical ship punched through the side of the station as it continued to break apart in space. At maximum burn, he navigated to the Randy Roger, which was clearly on his ship's sensors, flying away from his two original attackers.

Two, then three, then five blips appeared on the sensors, moving at him quickly. The attackers fired more missiles. The ship wouldn't make it to the Roger before they hit.

"I told you you'd never make it." The soldier laughed.

"What's your name?"

"My name is 'You're dead.'"

"Nice meeting you 'You're Dead.' Bye."

Halley engaged the pilot eject system. The next second he was launched into space. The following second, the sphere ship exploded. The next, Halley flew through space at maximum speed for the Roger. He wasn't going to let the cosmoship get away again.

◆ ◆ ◆

The cloaked Randy Roger was the size of a Nautilus-class base cruiser. Unlike a standard bridge, the lights were dim and a clear vertical display screen sat in front of its commander, Lazer, at his conn station.

The bald commander was abnormally muscular under his black augmented uniform up to the neck. His eyes were white—either optical implants or bionic eyes. He carefully watched a blip on the sensor board streaking to the Roger.

"Run or fire, commander?" one of the crew members asked.

"We don't run. We retreat," Lazer replied in a gruff voice. "Burn now."

"The other two ships are asking for instructions."

"Tell them to get back to the convoy as fast as they can and don't break comm silence again. We can handle this situation, if there's any situation to handle. Tell them we'll be right behind them."

"Telling them now, commander."

A sound popped above them at the moment their ship rapidly accelerated. Red lights flashed overhead.

"Commander, sensors say we have a punctured hull."

"Where?"

"Between Beta and Gamma sections, sir."

Lazer grinned. "I think we may have a guest."

"What, sir?" one of the crew asked.

"He's either hanging on the hull or already inside."

"Who?"

"Go find out."

◆ ◆ ◆

The corridor's lights had been increased to full illumination. A squad of copper-suited soldiers moved quickly in double column formation, armed with their thick rifles.

They stopped in their tracks. Their ears must have been playing tricks. The violent sounds unnerved and confused the men—loud hissing, growling, and spitting from two cats engaged in a fight to the death. The men knew there were no cats aboard the Roger.

"It's not real. Someone's running a psy-ops game on us. Keep moving forward," the platoon leader said from his position at the rear of the columns.

The platoon marched forward and stopped again. The

two column leads slowly peeked around the corner of the next corridor. Each raised a fist.

The platoon leader raced to the front and joined them. Around the corner about seven feet away were the bodies of two dead cats.

"They look real."

"They're not real. They can't be. Scan them."

"Nothing on scanners."

"Then get them and let's move forward."

The two column leads stared at him.

"What are you waiting for?"

"Just because our scanners don't show anything doesn't mean they can't be bombs or something."

"Are you saying we should wait here, held up by two fake furry cats? Here, I'll show you."

The platoon leader stepped into the center of the corridor and aimed his rifle. From the other end of the corridor, Halley appeared and shot him in the chest.

The two column leaders returned fire as the platoon leader crashed to the ground. The other squad members joined them, firing their rounds.

Halley shot the "dead cats." The corridor exploded.

♦ ♦ ♦

From his station chair, Commander Lazer watched the displays on his main vertical screen.

"Explosion on the Beta–Gamma corridor! We have eleven men down, commander!"

"Send more men," he said casually.

"Sending in reinforcements."

The explosive sound was unlike anything they had ever heard. All power blinked off for a second, then came back with red alert lights flashing. Lazer looked around but all displays were blank. The crew looked at him.

"Is the engine off?" he asked.

"Determining now, commander," one of the bridge officers said. Others joined him at his station.

"The engine's gone," said another from his corner station.

"What?" Lazer said.

He jumped up from his chair and ran out of the

Command room. The very end of the command deck corridor extended out and had bay windows fore and aft. Lazer looked at the window facing aft. The cloak had been disengaged and the ship was fully visible. Drifting behind them was the entire Gamma engine section! They had no propulsion.

Lazer looked at his bridge crew assembled around him. His rage began to well up within him.   He wanted to pound the windows, the walls, someone, but none of that would solve his problem.

"Commander!" a voice yelled from within the command room.

The men ran back onto the bridge.

"Someone's accessing the cargo hold," said the officer at the Internal Watch Station.

Lazer gritted his teeth and marched to his station. He pulled the magnetized mega-rifle from the side.

"Four men with me." He pointed at one of the crew members. "Send Blue Platoon and Red Platoon to meet us there ASAP!"

◆ ◆ ◆

Halley tried again but his interface wouldn't open the door. From his scans, the door and wall were a good foot long of steel alloy. The cargo hold was made to keep things in and prevent access by those who didn't have the right codes. He could hear the pitter-patter of their approaching boots on the steel plate floors coming down their corridor in the deck above.

Lazer came out of the lift with his four crewmen. Waiting for them were seventy soldiers at the entrance to open the hatch to the steps heading below deck.

"Men! We're going to make this quick. It's only one damn Earth Alliance soldier. Roadhouse!"

"Yes, sir."

"You take your platoon down and around."

"Yes, sir."

"Casino!"

"Yes, sir."

"You take your platoon down and straight through."

"Yes, sir."

"Men! We go on a count of—"

Halley flew up from the access stairs below and shot Lazer, Roadhouse, and Casino in their chests. As the men flew back, their chests exploding from the rounds, Halley engaged the entire squad with machine-gun fire. None of them knew what had hit them.

◆ ◆ ◆

Halley hit the call box on the wall at the junction. "Bridge, are you reading me?"

"Who's this?"

"Who's the senior officer there?"

"Who's this? Identify yourself."

"Bridge, I want you to open the cargo hold so I can rescue the Uroboros crew. Do that now."

"Who is this?"

"Are you opening the cargo hold?"

"No. Where's the commander?"

"The commander is dead, so if you're the senior officer on the bridge, then you're the commander. I'm telling you again to open the cargo hold so I can rescue the hostages."

"You can't kill us all."

Halley had moved in time. He'd heard the low breathing of a new soldier coming. Apparently, this one had a sniper rifle.

The sniper pulled himself back around the corner. His helmet had a squiggly camera so that, with the wire, he could see around the corner without exposing his body. He had missed his chance. The entire deck was littered with bodies, including the commander, who lay lifeless with his helmet blown off and his white eyes wide open.

He moved. Lifting the steel plate from one section of the floor, he climbed down into the crawlspace. He'd find the intruder from there. The moment he closed the floor plating, settling down on his hands and knees, the thermal signature of the intruder was gone. Nothing on motion sensors, nothing on thermals, nothing on audio.

Tap! Tap!

Someone was tapping on the steel-plated floor, maybe ten feet away around the corner.

Tap! Tap!

It was closer but still around the corner in the

adjacent corridor. He slowly shifted his body to lie flat on the floor of the crawlspace and then folded his rifle. He aimed it.

Tap! Tap!

The sound was in his section of the corridor, not more than four feet away. He aimed in the direction of the sound but where were the next taps going to come from? Three feet, two feet away, or right above him? The sniper realized that maybe the intruder could see his thermals.

He screamed out and began firing his rounds through the floor as he stood, pushing open the crawlspace with his head. Nothing. The same bodies of his comrades on the floor. He looked all around then stepped out of the crawlspace and onto the floor. He looked around the corner for the intruder and caught one round in the chest from Halley's rifle.

♦ ♦ ♦

"Bridge, I'm back. Are you reading me?" Halley said into the call box.

He could hear cursing on their end.

"Who are you?" the bridge officer asked.

"Bridge, open the cargo hold so I can rescue the Uroboros crew."

"No."

"That's it. No. That's your response. I wanted to do this the easy way, but you want me to come to the bridge. Then that's what I'll have to do."

"We're waiting for you."

"Then I won't keep you waiting."

The remaining bridge crew had the command room in complete lockdown with its reinforced barrier. A dozen mercenaries were in complete panic.

"Why are you pissing him off? He killed the commander and the others! What do we do?"

"Who's commander? Lazer's dead."

"Don Juan is commander."

Don was one of the youngest of the crew mercenaries, but he wasn't pacing or upset like the others.

"What do we do, commander?" one asked. Every one

of them stared at him, waiting for orders.

"If he took out the commander, Red and Blue Platoons, then we're not going to do any better. First, we stay in here and don't leave for any reason. I remember lots of people, including in this room, saying how weak-ass Earth Alliance is. Do we still feel that way?"

Everyone remained quiet until one finally said, "We got to take this guy down."

"No, we got to stay alive and wait for the rest of the convoy to get here."

"The convoy isn't coming back for us. We were heading to them."

"They'll come back."

"No, they won't and you know it. It's up to us to deal with this guy."

"He's not just one guy. He's Earth Alliance, some Marine or special ops."

"We know what he wants," Don said.

The men looked at each other. No one spoke for a while.

"Give him what he wants and he goes away."

"And what will our people do to us?"

"They aren't barricaded in the Control Room with this killing machine hunting us. He's already rendered the ship useless. We're just a floating hunk of junk of a ship in space without a paddle."

"How did he do that? How could he know all our systems?"

"Our systems are the same design as his systems. He knows how to disable his, he can disable ours. Do we give him the cargo hold?"

"Command isn't a democracy, Don. You tell us."

"What the—!"

Everyone turned to see what one of the crew members was staring at through the bay observation windows. Floating in space like an avenging angel was Halley in his super-suit.

He floated forward to the glass and rested his glove on it. Then giant claws came out of his suit glove and scratched the glass like nails on a chalkboard. Though none of them had ever seen either, they winced as he did.

Don stepped forward, wildly waving his hands.

"You win! Giving you access to the—"

Halley was gone. He flew away, back over the front of their ship.

Don ran to the conn and overrode the cargo hold lockouts.

"Don, we can't stay here. Once he gets the prisoners…"

"We're dead," Don said. "Gentlemen, to the escape pods. Disco, it's up to you and me. Self-destruct. That will keep him focused and away from us."

"Agreed!" everyone said.

◆ ◆ ◆

Halley had already gotten back aboard the ship and returned to the Beta-Gamma junction. The plan was simple: Rescue the Uroboros crew, leave in whatever ships were in the docking bay, call in the cavalry" (meaning the Marines) for rescue, and, for him, get back to the Tyson. At least his butt wouldn't be touching the conn of this ship.

With one touch, the doors opened. He stood to the

side as the bay doors slid fully open.   In his audio, he could hear the low breathing of many, many people, but no one called out. He stuck his finger, fitted with a cam, around the corner. On his faceplate mini-display, he saw nothing except rows of containers.

The ceiling height of the outside corridor was about eight feet. The height of the inner cargo hold was twenty feet. It would take less than a minute. A big gamble, but he'd risk it to save the hostages.

He flew in like a rocket, straight for the ceiling and the cover behind the highest stack of containers. On the ground looking up at him were at least forty copper-suited soldiers pointing their heavy rifles at the hostages—hundreds of them, sitting on the floor. Some were the Uroboros crew, but there were many others.

"Come down here, whoever you are!" one of them yelled at him. "Or we'll open fire on all of them."

Halley, in his combat fatigues, ran out from behind ground containers and opened fire first from a long handgun. Hostages dove for the ground as he struck the first mercenary soldiers. Other hostages jumped to their feet and tackled the mercenaries.

The soldier lowered his weapon and watched. The mercenaries were completely overwhelmed by the hostages—disarmed, wrestled, or beaten to the ground despite their copper suits. As they were all subdued and secured to the ground, Halley walked through the crowd to a single man with graying hair—what little hair he had with his buzz-cut. The man watched him with a wide smile.

"Hey, Dad."

"How, how did you get here, son? Aren't you supposed to be near Saturn? How did you get here? I don't understand."

"They said my dad was in a small predicament, so I volunteered to handle it. Now that it's sorted, what's new?"

Halley's father burst out laughing with tears in his eyes and hugged his son.

"Warning, self-destruct has been activated! You have three minutes to evacuate the ship!" the computer voice said.

Everyone froze.

Chapter Twenty

Every Third Sunday of June

Everyone crowded around Halley. He knew the Uroboros crew from their uniforms but that was about half of the hostages. He'd have to wait.

"Isn't there another landing bay here?" he asked them.

"No, they converted this to a brig. Their main docking bay is in the engine section. Why aren't we running there now?"

"Because they don't have an engine section anymore."

"What do you mean?"

They saw the concern in his face. "How many of you are there?"

"Over two hundred of us," one answered.

Halley's expression said it all: They had no means to escape the ship. "We need to stop the self-destruct ASAP." Halley signaled his super-suit and it descended. He was fully encased in less than a minute. "Talk to me, people."

"I can give it a shot," said a man who looked like a tech, based on his uniform.

"Warning, self-destruct has been activated! You have two minutes to evacuate the ship!"

"Sir, there is no 'giving a shot,'" Halley told the man. "In about two minutes, we'll all be dead in a great explosion in space, which will make all the work I did to rescue you for nothing."

"I can do it," said another man. Halley had a better feeling about him, though he wasn't one of the Uroboros crew.

"Then you and me, sir, are literally the only hope this group has. Are you sure?"

"I'm positive."

Halley was back in his super-suit, standing seven feet tall as he fitted on his helmet. He grabbed the man and they were gone.

Halley held the man at his waistline as they jetted down corridors, through open hatches, and up stairwells. He let him drop to his feet as he punched the outside button and the door opened.

"Warning proximity alert! Imminent collision in ninety seconds!"

"Warning, self-destruct has been activated! You have one minute to evacuate the ship!"

The man looked Halley with his mouth hanging open.

"Don't look at me! Go to work!

The man ran to the conn, looked on the console, and didn't see what he wanted. Then he ran to the Sensors station. Halley flew straight to Tactical. He saw an object on the sensors. It was the Bodacious Betty! He didn't know if the Randy Roger was floating to the Betty or vice versa, but he had to do what he thought the other cloaked ships had already done—blast it out of space.

"Found it!" the man said.

Halley aimed the weapons but paused. He looked at the object on the screen closely and did some quick calculations in his head. "I'm waiting on you!"

"Self–destruct has deactivated," the computer called out, to their relief.

"What are you waiting for?" the man asked him.

"No need to destroy it if we can hitch a ride."

"Hitch a ride. Why?"

Halley looked at him. "There may be more cloaked ships out there."

"A shield."

"And maybe, if we're lucky, a means of propulsion until the cavalry gets here."

Halley fired. The wrecked Bodacious Betty came into view across the main observation bay window. A flash of an explosion. The man wasn't sure if they were tilting up or the other ship was tilting down, but there was no collision. Halley fired station weapons again.

"Proximity alert canceled!" the computer announced.

"I'd say we'll be allowed to join the others, since we did our hero work for the day," the now smiling man said.

The main command doors opened and the Uroboros

crew and the other former hostages filed in.

Halley said, "Almost. I'm going to escort you back to the cargo hold, then I'll be spacewalking again to lasso that ship and ensure our ship-to-ship tether holds."

"No need," a familiar voice said. Halley turned to see his father walking toward him. "How do I get one of these s-suits?" He patted the arm of the suit.

"I'll see what I can do."

Halley took notice of the non-Uroboros crew. "Who are you?"

"We're with the Federation."

The men couldn't hear him sigh within his suit. "How did you end up here?"

"Same as them. We were kidnapped from our ship."

"Ship?"

"Yes. The Federation has cosmoships, too. Who, may I ask, are you? You did rescue us."

"Captain Halley. USS Army. Earth Alliance."

"You mean Planet Tamers," the Federation man said.

"That too."

"Captain." Anslem Halley stood on his tip-toes to pat his shoulder. "It's about time!"

"Yes, Captain Halley," the Federation man said. "We want to know who you are, too, so that in my report to my superiors, I'll know who to thank properly. Your superiors should know. Maybe more rank is in your near future."

"I hope not," Halley said.

"Don't be silly, Josh. Why shouldn't you be at the top of the food chain?" Halley's father said.

"Where are those prisoners?"

"They'll be remaining in the cargo hold until the cavalry arrives," a crew member said.

"Captain Halley, I'm sure your presence will be required again when Earth Alliance and the Federation decide how to respond to these Umbra criminals. There will be much fall-out back home about them."

"I'm no fan of Umbra, sir, but I don't think these mercenaries are Umbra."

The Federation crew looked at each other. "Why would you say that?" one asked. "We've been their prisoners for over a month."

"Who are the Homesteaders?" Halley asked.

The Federation members didn't answer.

"What do they have to do with this, whoever they are?" an Uroboros crew member asked.

"My point is that there are a lot of people out here in deep space all of a sudden and we need to find out who is who before we start making any hasty decisions and snap actions. But I'll leave all that to you. I need something to write with and some paper."

"Paper?"

"Yes, paper. Find it and something to write with."

"We can manage that."

"Secure the bridge, the command corridor, and—"

"Captain Halley, we know exactly what to do, including how to find your paper and pen."

"I'll go do my spacewalk, then."

◆ ◆ ◆

Halley did more than ensure the steel alloy tether connecting the two ships was secure. He had to board the derelict Betty. Most of its sections were open to space and not a soul was left within her. However, the bridge controls remained functioning. He powered up the engines and set its course back to Earth Alliance MAB territory. The Roger would be towed along. Betty and Roger arm in arm for likely their last voyage.

Halley returned to the Roger. EA and Federation crews had it locked down tight. Armed guards were in the corridors, and in the bridge all stations were manned. They had made contact with Command and help was on the way. EA had dispatched two Marine Barracudas.

The crew watched Halley take a sheet of paper and fold it a few times. It was an amusing sight to see a seven-foot suited soldier do arts and crafts at a bridge station. For a good fifteen minutes, he was writing and drawing. No one could make out exactly what he doing. He seemed to finish, then set down everything, and removed his helmet. Halley set the helmet on the table he was working at and marched to his father, who was as curious as the others.

"Hey, Dad, since I was busy with all this, I didn't get a chance to stop by the store, so I had to go old-school. You always did say important things are made with one's hands. Here it is, Dad. Happy Father's Day."

Anslem Halley stood there with an expression that looked like shock mixed with an open-mouthed smile. He looked at the makeshift card and slowly took it from his son.

"I'm supposed to be the one who forgets the holidays. Every third Sunday of June, sir."

"Sorry, I was a bit busy myself that last month."

Josh hugged his father.

Men on the bridge playfully said all together, "Awww!"

"We have Command online," the crew member at Comms said. "They're asking for you, captain."

Father and son let go of their embrace.

"That's the second time in a day you almost made me cry," Halley's father said.

"Captain, you can take it from the conn," the same crew member said.

Halley marched to the conn and shook his head. "Send it through," he said as he planted his butt in another command chair, that wasn't the Tyson's.

EPILOGUE

The NCS Neil deGrasse Tyson. Flagship of the Earth Alliance. Five months from Titan.

Capt. Ayla received the classified report code-named "Father's Day" from Admiral Antares. After reading it in her cabin, she convened an emergency meeting with both Navy and Army officers and enlisted command staff in her private captain's mess.

The Tyson had been on alert status for thirty-six continuous days.

♦ ♦ ♦

Crew were on guard outside, like the rest of the corridor and the rest of the Roger. Halley stepped into the private quarters and sat at his desk. He touched the flashing button next to the tilted in-desk screen.

Captain Ayla's smiling face stared back at him

"Hello, Navy," Halley greeted.

"Army," she said. "Should I get the command staff?"

"No, there's time for that later."

"Congratulations on rescuing your father and the Uroboros Station crew."

"Thank you."

"Everyone was praying and pulling for you."

"Thanks."

"And congratulations, Captain. I'm feeling much more secure about you now that you've come to your senses."

"I thought you'd say that."

"And what is this report of yours sent to me from the Admiral called 'Father's Day'? That's not standard naming protocol for an intel report. But I see you're prominently featured in it from top to bottom."

"Cloaked ships, captain," Halley said.

"We saw that. We've been on General Quarters ever since you left. We're ready to fire at anything within a nanosecond's notice. We're still not over what happened to the KCS Uju Kauboi and that report. What's not in this report?"

"Quite a bit, actually. Do you know that the Copernicus is ahead of schedule?"

"Yes, the Admiral notified me."

"I mean really ahead of schedule."

"You mean in the MAB."

"Yes."

"Your report says the Federation is out here, too. What do the One World freaks want?"

"HB, there's a lot of players out here. That's what worries. We've gone from being the only ones out here for four hundred million clicks in any direction on our merry way to Titan to a virtual cluster."

"I see you're not above making waves too. Command believes Umbra is involved but you said no."

"Why would Umbra get involved in this? Makes no sense. I saw them. Killing their own people. Opening fire on their own ships to get me. Mercenaries might not be military but they have a code of conduct too. These were thugs who couldn't care less about each other."

"Real mercenaries, then. All about the money."

"Criminals is what they were."

"What else did they say or do for you to think it's not Umbra? You were pretty emphatic in the report."

"They were speaking melange."

"You do know what you're saying, then?"

"Yes. I do."

"Someone or some people with the resources on par with Planet Tamers, the Federation, and Umbra. You're right. Things are getting crowded out here in deep space for us."

"I think we're going to have some serious problems ahead."

"Based on this report, I'd say you're right. Not to hurt your feelings but I asked the Admiral to assign me a larger Marine detachment. He said he already did. Also, he said you and the Marines bumped into each other multiple times on this mission. Seems like you impressed them again. The Admiral said it'll likely be them."

"Yes, if it's the ones I met, we couldn't do better."

"Good. They have your recommendation. I'll let them join up."

"Did they send all the telemetry from these cloaked ships, too?"

"All of it and we're poring over it all."

"One of the thugs called the technology 'visual occlusion.'"

"Cute. More like a distortion envelope of energy."

"I want you to look for any signs of it in your vicinity at all times."

"Copy that. We may have detected something."

"What?"

"Something ahead of us."

"Ahead? Where ahead?"

"On Titan."

"What? There's no one ahead of us."

"One of your soldiers spotted a blip on Titan."

"Impossible."

"I still say we'll be the first ones on Titan. The first humans on Titan. Earth Alliance. No one else. But after this report of yours and the last with the Kauboi, I'm letting my paranoia run wild and fancy-free."

"The Titan Project is fifty years in the making. No one is getting there ahead of us. No one else is terraforming that moon for the first time in human history. We've spent all our careers for this moment. No one's cutting in front of us."

"Agreed."

"Contact the SETI people on Earth."

"We're looking for extraterrestrials now?"

"No. We're looking for cloaked ships or any other blips in space around Saturn and Titan, or on Titan. I agree with you. We should be worrying."

"The report said the hostiles who kidnapped your father and the Uroboros crew said they had a convoy. A convoy of cloaked ships ahead. The Admiral wanted to make sure we were on alert status with weapons ready."

"Five months to go. That's it."

"I still believe this is Umbra or even the Federation. They can't do it, so they're trying to sabotage the mission."

"We've lived in space for many years. Served as officers for most of our adult lives. In all that time, never has there been an accident, death, or weapons fire ever. Let alone the crime of kidnapping and hostage-taking in space. All of that has happened in one month. We have five months to go before we get to Titan. When we land, we'll be two years from Earth. A lot of things can happen in two years if we're not the only ones out here. "

"Then when can the Tyson expect your return, Army?"

"I'll be on my way back tomorrow."

"We'll hold down the fort in the meantime."

♦ ♦ ♦

__THE PLANET TAMERS__ Military Sci-Fi Series continues ...

Join my <u>VIP Readers' Club</u> to find out when Book Two in the series releases!

In the meantime, check out either my *Liquid Cool* series or my *Fabled Quest Chronicles*.

REVIEW REQUEST

Dear Reader,

I hope you enjoyed *Father's Day*. <u>**Can You Write Me a Review?**</u>

If you enjoyed ***Father's Day (A Military Sci-Fi Planet Tamers Novel)***, I'd greatly appreciate an honest review on one or more of the following sites:

  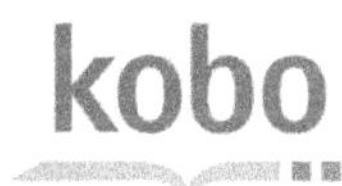

Reviews are the best way for readers to discover good books. My writer's motto is simple: "Readers Rule!" Thanks so much.

Always writing,

Austin Dragon

Don't forget to Join My Exclusive **VIP Readers' Club**!

My fiction universe includes Epic Fantasy, Sci-Fi and more. Your benefits include free books, the latest announcements, special offers and fun giveaways. You can unsubscribe at any time.

Sign up Today and get FOUR of my full-length novels **FREE**! Join HERE!

Always writing,

Austin Dragon

ABOUT THE AUTHOR

Austin Dragon is the author of over 20 books in science fiction, fantasy, and classic horror. His works include the sci-fi detective _LIQUID COOL_ series, the epic fantasy _FABLED QUEST CHRONICLES_, the international futuristic epic _AFTER EDEN_ Series, the classic _SLEEPY HOLLOW HORRORS_, and the new _PLANET TAMERS_ military sci-fi series. He is a native New Yorker but has called Los Angeles, California home for more than twenty years. Words to describe him, in no particular order: U.S. Army, English teacher, one-time resident of Paris, ex-political junkie, movie buff, Fortune 500 corporate recruiter, renaissance man, futurist, and dreamer.

He is currently working on new books and series in science fiction, fantasy, and classic horror!

http://www.austindragon.com/books

***